PRAISE FOR *THE CAUSATIVE FACTOR*

"Suspenseful, original, and full of heart, this novel gripped me from the first page and continued to surprise me throughout. What does it mean to make a life, to make art, to make a life making art? I'll always remember these characters and their complex paths."

—Andrea Barrett, National Book Award winner, *Natural History*

"I couldn't stop turning the pages of Megan Staffel's *The Causative Factor*. Her characters are so vivid and so complicated and their lives are full of exhilarating surprises as they try to shape the future and negotiate the past. A spellbinding novel."

—Margot Livesey, author of *The Boy in the Field*

"Early on in Megan Staffel's beautiful new book, there's talk of art that 'proves the extraordinary is out and about in the world.' *The Causative Factor* is just that proof. Haunting, stirring, and bracingly romantic, this is a novel to fall head over heels for."

—Liam Callanan, author of *When in Rome*

"Megan Staffel writes as gorgeously and movingly about the psychological legacies that inform our choices as she does about the way in which art and a deep attunement to nature allow us to create ourselves anew. Staffel tells us that 'the smallest acts matter' and in this astute and embracing novel, she shows us the ways in which a dab of paint on a canvas, or the movement of water in a stream, can change lives."

—Marisa Silver, author of *The Mysteries*

"Megan Staffel's compelling new novel follows Rachel and Rubiat as they embark on a project that lasts long past college. As desires collide, splinter, and realign, Staffel deftly weaves a startling, artful story of how to make a life."

—Tara Deal, author of *Life/Insurance*

"Megan Staffel's *The Causative Factor* is a singular, exquisitely written story of love sundered by circumstance and misunderstanding."

—Peter Selgin, author of *A Boy's Guide to Outer Space*

THE CAUSATIVE FACTOR

Megan Staffel

Regal House Publishing

Published by
Regal House Publishing, LLC
Raleigh, NC 27605
All rights reserved

ISBN -13 (paperback): 9781646034932
ISBN -13 (epub): 9781646034949
Library of Congress Control Number: 2023950615

Cover images and design by © C. B. Royal
Author photo by Brian Oglesbee

Let It Be Me (Je T'appartiens)
English Words by Mann Curtis
French Words by Pierre Delanoë
Music by Gilbert Becaud
Copyright © 1955, 1957, 1960 FRANCE MUSIC COMPANY Copyrights Renewed
All Rights for the U.S. and Canada Controlled and Administered by
UNIVERSAL MUSIC CORP. All Rights Reserved Used by Permission

Reprinted by Permission of Hal Leonard LLC
Regal House Publishing, LLC
https://regalhousepublishing.com

Printed in the United States of America

For the witness

Was there anything important, anything that would provide some sort of reason or clue to what happened next? Lois can remember everything, every detail; but it does her no good.

—Margaret Atwood, "Death by Landscape"

PART ONE

PARTNERS

1

The class meets on the top floor of an empty house the university no longer maintains. They are artists in the making and the filthy surroundings suit them more than a normal classroom. The stairs are slanted, the windows leaky, and spiderwebs and mouse droppings are everywhere. In the bathrooms the plumbing is noisy, the faucets rusted. Rubiat, one of the most vocal members of the class, christens it "Gothic." Someone else says, "haunted."

At first, it's Rubiat she notices. He's thin and tall, and dresses in bright colors. There's always a red scarf wrapped around his neck, boots on his feet that strike the wooden floors loudly. She finds him pretentious.

The man she's taken by is their teacher Denton, a dancer, actor, artist from England. He's at their school for only a semester as an artist in residence and this is his only class. Called *Body Expression*, it's a practicum in Performance Art, a new and popular discipline at their art school.

Denton seems barely older than they are, and there's a sly, restrained quality about him she likes, as though he's enjoying his own private joke which he might, or might not, reveal. He speaks to them as friends, and the fact that he'll be making the final judgment and giving the grade is irrelevant. He tells them this. What's important is experience. He wants them to have a full, immersive experience. He wants them to lose themselves in work. Work, he tells them, is sacred, it is a way of communicating their deepest thoughts and feelings, a way of telling the world who they are and what they know. He makes these statements as he walks up and down in the long, windowed room at the top of the house, his jagged blond hair and blue-jeaned figure moving in and out of the light. They are mesmerized. He has an intensity that feels, on its own, like the definition of an artist. It's something Rachel hopes to achieve, and it starts with a determination to be bold, to embody purpose, to speak clearly and directly about the human spirit.

In September, Denton lectures. He lays out the history of performance art, showing how it developed from Dadaism, a movement that celebrated the irrational. Denton shows them old footage of performances from the Café Voltaire in Zurich. They discuss the dancing (mimicking machines), the music (atonal, unmelodic), the costumes (playful and childish), and the spectacle of adults dismantling the scaffolding of reason as a way to protest the atrocities of the First World War. They create their own performances, using materials they find in the house—pots, lampshades, curtains, silverware—and it all ends in laughter. Dadaism takes them to surrealism, where the focus moves into sculpture and painting, while still maintaining loyalty to the irrational. Denton shows them how the surrealists celebrated disorder, taking familiar objects out of their normal contexts and putting them into new and strange juxtapositions. They play Exquisite Corpse, marveling at what can happen when control is removed from the creative act.

Rachel likes going back in time to see how it all started. And she likes the drama of Denton's beautiful English voice in the dark room as he projects one painting after another that proves the extraordinary is out and about in the world. All a person has to do is loosen the order of things. For viewing films and projections, they move from the light-filled room at the top of the house to a dark, shuttered kitchen, large enough for rows of folding chairs.

In October they begin long-term projects. Denton pairs them in what seems like a spontaneous and arbitrary manner, though later, she will wonder. When he says Elsayem/Goodwin she sees Rubiat look around the room. Rachel knows Elsayem is Rubiat's last name and she suspects that when he discovers she's Goodwin, he will feel the same disappointment.

Their assignment is to identify their partner's essential quality.

"Describe it in words and then find a way, without using props or costumes, to express it through movement." Denton takes them back down to the kitchen to show them film footage of dancers, actors, comedians and invites them to steal any move that might be useful. "Your objective is to know your partner intimately. And by the way, I'm not suggesting sex." Everyone laughs. "That's your choice of course." A tiny smile crosses his face. "But talking can also achieve intimacy. Interview them. But it's not really facts you're interested in; you want to find their deepest motivation, the hidden foundation of their character, that quality that makes them the person they are. That's what you're after. We'll call it the causative factor, the one characteristic emotion from which their words and actions derive. The surprising thing is that your partner might not even know what it is. Or, in the end, you might disagree with what they identify as the thing you're looking for. So, beware. This is your vision, but for it to be an honest one, it must be free of flattery or disapproval. You are not critiquing, you are representing and expressing, removing your partner from their usual context, uncovering the emotion they are grounded in. Is it fear, anger, sympathy? Is it joy or grief? You might even ask yourself: What animal are they? What animal do they remind you of? And by the way, there is film footage of animals in the library. That can be a resource."

The image that accompanies his words is engraved in her memory: a slight, blond-haired man standing in front of a monstrous kitchen range. He grasps the stove railing, and the oven door falls open, the black maw of its grease-encased interior facing them, mice scuttling into view, and just as quickly, disappearing.

Matching Rubiat's stride is difficult. He has long legs, and his boots are loud even on the sidewalk. He says he wants to drop his books off in his room, so he will meet her at the dining hall. That's a relief because she can walk the rest of the way in silence. Rachel lives off campus, too far to drop off books.

They make her backpack heavy, but she was on the swim team in high school and has the shoulder muscles to carry it.

Rachel follows the stream of students entering a modern glass and steel structure that rises, improbably, from a sloping lawn fringed by old brick buildings. It's an old campus, nestled in the hills of the western part of New York State. The original buildings are modest. They feel connected with the landscape while the newer ones of modernist design stand out from it in garish, uncompromising ways. But Rachel loves the school, and the mixture of old with new is a chaos she thrives on. If "Body Expression" met in a traditional classroom, it wouldn't have the same power; the strangeness of the setting is, in itself, an inspiration.

She doesn't see Rubiat approach, though she's been looking out the windows the whole time. He must have come in the back way. He's wearing quiet shoes and has reached her table before she sees him. "Rachel."

"There you are! You snuck up on me. And you already have your food!"

"No worries, I'll wait."

She wonders about that. Why had he slipped in so mysteriously? But to start their project being suspicious would wreck it. She decides to let it rest, think of it as something born from his desire for drama.

When she returns with a tray of food, not nearly as much food as he has, there's an awkward silence. She settles into her seat, picks up her fork and says, "You're different at close range." What she means is that his height, probably more than six feet, his angularity, his coat-hanger shoulders, seem less imposing when he's seated.

She has always paid attention to men's facial hair: so many textures, shapes, colors it is a defining element. But Rubiat is clean shaven although his cheeks, at this hour, are shadowed. He bends to his food, his dark hair pulled into a ponytail. Clearly, he's not eager to begin, but finally he says, "How so?"

You're not so intent on being noticed is what she means, but she doesn't say that. She says instead, "I think you're a little unsure about this project. In fact, I'd say you're definitely not a Denton acolyte."

"Right, I'm hugely regretting this class."

He seems relieved to be able to admit this.

"Why?"

"It all seems forced. Turning what should be spontaneous expression into an academic study. Using all the ways the powerless take over space and speak to authority, like protests or street performance, stuffing it all into a course, it's bullshit. You lose the authentic, the inspiration of the moment. But, that said, I'm here. And if I'm here, I have to guard against my cynicism. So, I'm not going to ruin anything. Don't worry. You looked so worried." His lips curl into a half smile. His New York accent is foreign to her ears, making her realize he's a product of that sophisticated place, and maybe that's the source of his challenging tone.

"Tell me something, Rachel Goodwin. That's such a sturdy name, it's like a four-legged table. Do you have a middle name?"

"Normal. Don't laugh. It was my mother's maiden name."

"I find that very fitting. Because that's how I see you. And close up, you seem even more competent, more orderly, more confident than I thought. In fact, you're thoroughly intimidating."

"Sorry," she says.

"Oh no, it's nothing to apologize for. It's admirable. I'm a mess, in comparison. A bit spinning of the wheels in the snow sort of thing. If you know what I'm saying."

"I was always the person parents hoped their children would emulate."

"And I…" His voice trails off. "Well, you tell me."

"You're the guy girls got crushes on. But their parents didn't approve, did they?"

"Don't be fooled. The secret is, I aspire to be everything you represent, or at least, appear to represent. Wouldn't it be amusing if, in the long term, we turn out to be the opposite of what we seem? That I am, at heart, a pretty average guy? A plumber, maybe. That seems like the ideal life. You fix things; you make them work. You learn from a teacher, textbooks, and that's all you need. You're prepared for every possibility."

"If that's the ideal, why art school?"

"Exactly what my mother asked. And continues to ask, if you want to know the truth." He looks at the wall of windows. Then he looks down at her and his voice is softened, less declamatory. "I tell her I'm at the mercy of impulse. I'm sorry to disappoint her, but it controls me. And you? Why art school for you? You seem more destined for...well, you tell me."

"Doctor, lawyer, banker. I'm really good at math and science but it's all too logical. Nothing makes me feel so happy as the absurd."

"Really? Maybe you can give me an example. It seems so unlike you, or at least my initial sense of you." His pupils are layers of darkness.

Absurd. Such an easy word to toss around. But she needs its dislocation, its reversal of expectations. It fuels humor, sympathy, everything. "I once saw a woman do a performance about getting dressed to go out. She came onto the stage nude. And then she proceeded to clothe herself with the skimpiest, most provocative clothing, a skirt hardly any longer than, say, twelve inches, high-heeled shoes, stockings with garters that stretched down her thighs, you get the idea. The clothing, instead of covering her, made her more undressed than her nakedness which, in comparison, seemed thoroughly innocent and mild."

He's listening with his head cocked to the side, his entire body intent on her, and that's when she sees how beautiful he is, how utterly masculine and beautiful, and in a flash, she knows she will sleep with him. It's why she had chosen *that* as her illustration. She recognizes the other signs: flushed neck, loss of appetite. Desire is flooding her body and if she isn't careful, it will be communicated to him before she has any say in the matter.

"The artist wore a plastic female face that covered her own and the driving beat of the music contributed to the sense you had that this woman was being dutiful. She was obeying the norms, behaving in the way the culture told her she should. She was making herself attractive. Putting her body on view. That's what it meant to her. And that's what I mean by absurd, that dressed could be more undressed than nakedness."

"I like that! I wish I had seen it. Where did you see it?"

"Oh, it was last year sometime. She came here for a couple of weeks. Was a visiting artist for a while. You weren't here then?"

"I transferred in from another college. This is my first year."

"I didn't think I'd seen you around."

"I tried the plumbing thing."

"Literally?"

"No, not literally, but I went to community college. Didn't work out. And the impulse thing. I decided I'd better make use of it, otherwise I'd be doomed."

"So, what exactly do you mean, being at the mercy of impulse?"

"It's hard to describe. Let's see…"

"I mean, if it's not too personal."

"Nothing's too personal. Or rather, if it's too personal, it should be expressed because that's the most valid expression of all, right?"

"Right."

"It's really strong, when it comes on, it takes over. Everything, my body, my mind. And it's definitely something I shouldn't do. That's the thing, that's why I have to use it, otherwise it will destroy me."

"Are we talking, like, drugs?"

"No, I can't do drugs. Drugs, alcohol, I have to stay away from them. Because moderation is not in my vocabulary, if you get what I mean."

"Well, that's a good thing to know about yourself. So, when was the first time? Were you really young?"

"I had just learned to drive, so I was sixteen, and on the first day I had my license I got on the FDR. It was three in the morning. Me and a couple of friends; we'd been at a show. There wasn't much traffic, and I was going along regularly, until I noticed that the speedometer went up to 120, and it seemed unfortunate that the needle never went above seventy. That's fifty miles of speed unexperienced. I wanted to know what it felt like and realized that right then was the best opportunity, so I put my foot on the gas. Got to a hundred, but I missed a shift in lanes and slammed into poorly lit construction. The car was totaled, but no one was hurt. It's like someone dares me and I can't say no."

"Wow, that's serious."

"Right. So, what about you? What is your most wild thing? What is the thing that most frightens you, or shames you maybe?"

She smiles. "I don't think I know you well enough to tell you about that."

"Can you give me a hint?"

"Let's see, okay, it has to do with contradiction."

"Right," he says thoughtfully.

While they've been talking, the dining hall has emptied out. Work-study students in long white aprons are collecting dishes, wiping tables. In a far corner, they're putting chairs up so they can sweep and wash the floor.

Rachel shares a house in the village of Crandall with five other people. It's a short walk from the campus on a street of single-family homes, old maple trees shading their yards. From the outside, the large white clapboard house looks well-kept. The trash cans are neatly stored in the back, and though the interior has been broken up into separate rooms, the classic nineteenth-century exterior is still an icon of respectability. It's a two-story house, like all the others in the village, but there is a cupola that contains a single room. That's Rachel's. She opens her door and walks into the darkness, telling Rubiat to wait in the hallway. The lamp is on the other side of her room and when she switches it on, she notices her bra on the bed and whisks it into a drawer.

"Nice place," he says, entering just as soon as she turns around.

"A friend of mine had this room last year, so when she left, I grabbed it." There are windows in all directions and though it's night now, she tells him that sunrise and sunset are spectacular and even on a cloudy day she can see all the way to the surrounding hills.

She plugs in her electric kettle, makes them cups of tea. He stretches out on the rug, his legs extending the length of it and his feet, now that he's taken off his shoes, are long too. His socks don't seem very clean, and they're too thin to protect much from the cold. He leans against her desk; she leans against the bed, facing him.

"This is cozy," he says. "I was thinking maybe you could tell me about it here."

"What?" But she's only stalling. She knows exactly what he means.

"Or maybe you could tell me about your childhood. Would that be possible?"

She describes for him the secure, orderly existence she'd had with two parents and a brother in a suburb of Rochester, which is only seventy miles north, close enough that she's able to return several times each semester and never feel that she's entirely left. He tells her it's the opposite for him. He's never met his father, and his mother, who is slightly crazy, lives in Manhattan, a day-long bus ride. They always spend New Year's and July Fourth together; they both like fireworks. Also, his birthday is the fourth and his present to her is that he comes home to celebrate it with her. "She calls me her happy accident."

"She sounds pretty wonderful. My parents, I'm sure, planned my arrival. It was exactly two years after my brother's."

"Your most wild thing?" he reminds her. "Or maybe, something you do that shames you, or even, maybe, frightens you?"

She's glad the light in the room is low, because she can feel the heat climb into her face with this question and wonders if he doesn't realize what's going on. Is he truly that oblivious? Or maybe he isn't interested in women. Maybe that should be one of *her* questions. He feels impossibly far away at this moment. She could, very easily, touch the end of his foot with her foot simply by flopping it over. Would that tiny touch ruin the comfortable feeling that has descended? Probably. "I'm feeling comfortable right now. Even though I don't know you, and that's pretty amazing."

"That's not an emotion."

"Love," she corrects.

"Lust?"

"I don't think they're so easily separated. At least in my experience. I'm feeling it really strongly in fact." Her foot flops over to touch his and she sees a mischievous smile pucker his lips. "The answer to that question?" She unbuttons her blouse, unhooks her bra, sits up straight, showing herself. "These are also who I am. This is my wildness."

The sky has darkened. They get rid of their clothing and since she made the first move, she continues with the same boldness. As though she is practiced at this, when the truth is, she must learn it over again each time, with each different person. With him, there's nothing awkward or hesitant, and as the rain slashes against the glass, her certainty grows. This is exactly what she wants to do.

They wake at dawn. He throws his leg over her, takes her face between his hands. His face is softened by sleep, his personality absent, so what she sees are two brown eyes focused on her. His voice is gentle. "I know you, don't I? I've studied you and I've seen what you need. You're a complicated puzzle, Ms. Goodwin, but I think I might have helped."

No one has ever claimed her like this. It feels a little creepy. It's intrusive as hell, blatantly paternalistic. But then she sees that his eyes have closed and from the regularity of his breath, she can tell he's fallen back to sleep. It was a message from his dreams, unedited. And, actually, he did help. She feels looser, happy; her correctness has been toppled over.

When they wake up later, the room is washed in light. His pretentiousness is gone. Without clothes, he's simply a tall, narrow man with long wavy hair. She loves his penis. It's the same, but different from the others she's seen up close, better, somehow.

They take turns in the bathroom, sneaking down the stairs in the still-sleeping house, standing under the hot water, toweling off with the pink towel, the one she tells him is hers. Back in the room he says, "I want to spend the whole day with you."

This isn't the person she'd imagined him to be.

"But not here, out in the world. I don't want to talk to people here. I don't want to go to studio. I want to take the day off. The two of us. That's what I want. Do you have a car? Could we go somewhere?"

That's when she knows they're lovers. She's never had a lover before. She's had sex partners, but never a lover. And if a lover is a person who wants to spend the whole next day with you, and only you, she will never settle for a sex partner again.

2

Rachel is a child of Rochester, a city in western New York State that is surrounded by gorges. Each one has been turned into a park, and the Rochester public schools take their students on day trips to visit them. Time is more visible in these places. Centuries of wind and water have cut channels through cliffs of shale, creating dramatic heights and waterfalls. And with them, the lesson of constancy, proof for any who take notice, that the smallest acts matter. As a child, Rachel might have understood this, and especially because her family often camped at the park where they are headed. Letchworth Park is southwest of the city, Watkins Glen southeast, and Stony Brook is southcentral. The WPA built these parks and the stone walkways, steps, bridges, all of it constructed in the 1930s, have endured.

At one time a railroad trestle spanned the gorge at Stony Brook and the huge structures that held the missing tracks are still there. She tells him these things when they are in the car. Stony Brook is her favorite gorge and she wants him to appreciate it. He's a relaxed passenger, listening, watching the landscape, knees up against the dashboard, head brushing the roof. After last night, this closeness feels easy.

They stop at a farm market and buy dates and apples for breakfast. They kiss between sips of coffee, bites of apple. She wants him all over again, but when she suggests it, he says, "Sorry, I'm done." It might have hurt, but he turns to her with a smile that erases the harshness of his words.

"For the time being," she adds, and in retrospect, she remembers that was *her* phrase. Seventeen hours total, from the time they left class to the bench at the farm market. She isn't sure the park will be open, but she remembers fall trips in elementary school.

"Missing tracks? I've always liked the word missing," he says, leaning back on the bench to get the sun on his face.

"Stony Brook is a smaller, more intimate park than the others. There's a path that runs next to the stream, past all the little pools where water collects, past the spills and waterfalls. In the summer, they dam the stream at the north end and make a huge swimming pool. There's a picnic area and a campsite and it's wonderful, swimming between rock walls. That's all WPA too, the patio and stone benches next to the pool so people can sit and watch. There's no diving though. It's not allowed and that always used to frustrate me as a kid. I loved diving. In high school, I was on the swim team. At one point, I thought I might become a professional."

"That's interesting. I was a diver too."

"Really? I would have thought you'd be on the basketball team."

"All tall men play basketball. Right. Well, I liked to dive."

"It's a really weird sport. I mean, it's so hard."

"Right. It's terrifying, it's the ultimate challenge of humanity because it's so against our nature. We're not birds, after all. Were you really advanced? How many years did you do it?"

"Four years, but I was always better in the back dives. I don't know, something about trust, or looking backward. I was really excellent at back dives."

"I don't know that I could do any of them excellently. But it was the somersaults that were hard for me because of my height. Just doing one was difficult. I liked the plain forward dive, knifing into the pool."

"Yeah, I loved the feeling of hitting water. But I loved all of it: the echo of voices around the pool, the changing room with locker doors slamming, standing under the showers in such a public way, nervous to show our bodies. Girls, that age, you know."

"What I craved, and it was a craving, was the privacy of it. See, that's what I didn't like about basketball. Too many people, too crowded. Our apartment was small and my mother is a large personality. But standing at the back of the board, preparing to dive, regardless of how many people were around, I was alone. I took my time. I waited for that certainty, that instant when everything is in play, irrevocably, then I went forward. You know what I mean, I'm sure."

"Interesting. I never thought of it that way. It wasn't so special. I just dove and dove. There were only seven people on the team. We had a pretty small school."

"My team was citywide and there were, let's see, there must have been maybe a hundred fifty divers total, which was a lot for each school. So, you had only a couple of chances."

She drops her empty cup into the trash, gathers their things. The market is crowded now. "Ready?" Later, she will wish they had stayed longer. Because she might have said that the best thing about diving was how you pushed yourself. You competed with yourself and you were never satisfied, never good enough. The water just bounced you back to the surface to try again. Nothing was ever final.

She pays the entrance fee, drives to the parking lot. For a Saturday, there aren't many cars. The grass is covered with leaves from the storm last night. He keeps his scarf wrapped around his neck, and his green pants, so odd everywhere else, blend with the landscape. She pulls a knit hat over her head, buttons her jacket. She wears lace-up shoes with ridged soles, but he has only sneakers. Nothing on his soles to grip and the skim of ice on the rocks hasn't melted.

There are two trails, the gorge trail along the stream, and the rim trail that climbs to the top of the cliff. In the summer, most people take the lower trail because once out of sight of park officials, people like to do exactly what all the signs prohibit: walk and splash in the creek. Now, only the rim trail is open. The gorge trail is too narrow, too icy and slippery from fallen leaves.

The ascent is steeper than she remembers. The steps have short risers and he is ahead of her, taking two at a time. She's breathing hard. The cold makes her nose run; she wipes it on her glove when she's sure he isn't looking, but when she catches up to him, he hands her a tissue from his pocket. It embarrasses her. The sun comes through the trees at a slant. Everything glistens. So many leaves on the ground, but some still hanging from the branches, yellow tassels glinting in the light.

"It's so beautiful," she says, pausing to get her breath.

"Let's not name it anything."

"That's an odd thing to say."

"What I mean is, let's just feel it, not judge it. Does a bird judge a lizard? Maybe that's the difference between us and them." He sits down on a step. "Here's the fox's point of view. What does he see? Smell?"

She sits down too. "Leaves, earth, stone. I think all those things have a smell if you're an animal."

He puts his arm around her, pulls her close. "What's the word you would use to describe me?"

She has forgotten about the assignment. Hasn't love taken them beyond it? Beyond words? "Vigorous?" She laughs, presses into him. "And me?"

He looks at her then, but not at her face. He unbuttons her jacket, looks at her breasts. He leans his head against her sweater. "Comfortable. Like I've found my place." And then a non sequitur: "The other thing about diving? It was the one time I was in control. Completely. No interruptions. I determined the end result. Preparing, and then going forward, totally committed, every muscle in my body ready."

Vigorous and *comfortable*, meaningless words when you thought about the entirety of a human being and all the barriers to truly knowing them. No, vigorous wasn't the right word for him. Control was a clue. How about *combative*? She doesn't say this, but she's aware of a slight friction, like he's not only watching, but fighting her in secret ways. He doesn't ever just submit. And of course, for him, that's why comfort would be important.

They have almost gained the top. The waterfall is close, but she won't tell him, she wants it to be a surprise. This is where the great concrete pillars that once held the train tracks stand. They are ugly; the cement is pitted from wind and ice and covered with moss. A chain-link fence runs along the edge of the cliff, but it's only waist high. They lean against it looking down at the black ribbon of stream far below. The roar of the waterfall is discernible, but only if you know it's there, otherwise you'd think highway. There's a sign for the campground where her family used to come for vacation. The bathrooms would be closed, but she walks in their direction, looking for a place where she can squat in privacy and pee. Crouching behind beautiful (there it is again) leafy bushes, she looks around, enjoying the fox's view. This outing is a good thing to do, a nice break from studio.

When she finds her way back to the path, he isn't there. Of course, he's gone on ahead. He would have wanted to find the source of the sound. She climbs to the peak and there it is, a spectacular plunging of water, more ferocious because of last night's rain. Not quite Niagara Falls, but not bad for Rochester. Yet Rubiat isn't in sight. Wouldn't he have waited? She runs ahead, thinking that maybe he has gone on, but sees no one. Maybe he, too, went off to pee and is waiting for her below, so she backtracks. But he isn't there either. Maybe he was taking longer. Best to wait, he was bound to show up soon. She sits on a stone. But she doesn't like the hulking presence of the useless pillars. Standing up, she feels better. Walks to the fence and looks over. Those green pants, the red scarf around his neck. She turns her head and sees a splash of red, the scarf is coiled on the ground, his sneakers next to it. Through the trees she sees him standing at the edge of the cliff, barefoot, poised for a dive. He is preparing to dive as though he's standing on the edge of a board, as though it will spring him upward. But it doesn't. He rises on his own incredible height and energy. Absurd. He's in the air, head between arrowed arms, legs together, feet pointed, diving into a rush of green, disappearing.

The sound in the air is from *her* throat, not his. It's a cry that fills the enormity of the damp October day.

3

The parking lot is washed in a blaze of pulsing red lights. The ambulance keeps its motor running, the cruisers' doors are flung open, radio static filling the air, and officials dressed in black, with ominous objects hanging from their belts, stand in twos and threes. She walks them to the spot while the EMTs follow along the lower trail with a stretcher. The scarf and the sneakers are still there. She asks if she can take them. The scarf is silk and badly stained, the sneakers are size thirteen, scuffed and worn out, impressions of his feet on the insoles.

When they don't find a body they call in air patrol. She has lost all sense of time because right away, it seems, there is a helicopter hanging in the sky, the swirling blades deafening. It swings along the upper reaches of the gorge, two men in the cockpit with binoculars. After it makes the first sweep through the gorge, it turns around and makes a second. Then she loses track, and when it finally flies off after hovering above the parking lot for excruciatingly loud minutes, a policewoman comes over to tell her it made five sweeps in all but saw nothing.

They decide to scour the other side of the stream. She goes with them, calling his name, though their loudspeakers do it better, Rubiat Elsayem! Rubiat Elsayem! But the high stone walls garble the sounds and as their powerful lights destroy the dim, leafy spots along the trail, it feels like a shoot for a movie. Standing, walking, waiting, she holds the tissue he gave her. It's something to connect them, but then the tissue falls onto the walkway, the afternoon passes, and they conclude he's not there, neither dead nor alive. The ambulance leaves first, then one of the cruisers.

The policewoman and her male partner put her in the back seat of the patrol car while they ask the same questions all over again, but she is trembling so violently she's useless. No, she hadn't known him long. Yes, she knows nothing, (or almost nothing) about his history. She did know that he had been on the diving team in his high school in New York. Her teeth chatter. "He was perfectly composed, like he was preparing to dive from a high board. We had talked about it. You see, I had been a diver too."

"New York City? That's where he was from?"

She can see their prejudices at work: rich people, entitled youth, druggies.

The female cop speculates. He wouldn't get far, he was barefoot, after all. Of course, someone might have given him a ride. "Maybe it was prearranged. A crazy prank. Get you ready for Halloween." They chuckle. The other officer says, "The best thing for you to do is go back to school and see if he shows up. Because he's not here. That we can be sure of." They take her number and give her a number to reach them if she thinks of anything else, and the female officer walks her back to her car, shutting her door when she's seated. She tells her to take it easy, she's had a terrible scare, and then she adds, speaking through the open window, leaning in so close Rachel can see streaks of makeup on her cheeks, "Some advice? He's not worth it. Don't waste any more emotion on this person who has played such a terrible trick on you. That's what I'd say if you were my daughter. They're always telling me, down at the station, Ricky, you're just a big old mama. And I am. You take care now."

She sits in her car until they leave. She can't get rid of the feeling that he's lying somewhere, hurt and immobile. But night is descending, and they scoured both sides of the gorge, from the air and from the ground, and found nothing. She opens her door, takes his shoes and scarf and walks to the lower trail, past the barriers, but it's too dark, and she goes only as far as the swimming area. She sets them down on the rock ledge gently. When, and if, he appears, she wants him to find them. If it was a joke, like the police believe, then he is heartless.

Her heat on high, radio blaring noisy rock music, she turns

right, toward Rochester, and shows up at her parents' house an hour later. They think she has the flu and put her to bed, where she stays for three days, shivering and vomiting, refusing food.

At school, his friends ask if she knows where he is. Denton refers to him as "MIA Rubiat" and pulls her aside to ask what she knows. Her instinct is to protect herself, so she tells him nothing, but when she realizes she's letting her desire for privacy prevent anyone from knowing the truth, it's too late to change the story. If it had only been a prank, then she is an idiot. A reporter for the *Dansville Gazette* gets her number from the police, but she pretends she isn't Rachel Goodwin and has never been to or even heard of Stony Brook.

And then there is the assignment. Her word had been *vigorous*. But that was because of sex. Vigorous wouldn't apply to the day after. Neither would kind, another word she had been thinking of. She pictures him standing at the edge of the cliff, body poised to go over. And then emptiness. He was a powerful, sly, cunning animal. Cruel. Feline or canine? Wolf, cougar, coyote? She attends classes, but she can't participate, it takes weeks for the shock to subside, and even then, she feels unfamiliar to herself, as though when he took his dive, he also took something essential of hers. She will never have it again, and maybe being more wary, less trusting is a good survival tool for a woman to have.

She goes to the library and locks herself in a viewing room with a set of videos on animal behavior. It's a Friday night; she can feel the campus seething with anticipation for the weekend. The library empties out around her but she is oblivious. A snake can disappear in the thinnest crevice of rock. It hides and then attacks. It eats mice, voles, rats, even smaller snakes, including those of its own species. It is pure antagonistic energy, yet despite its size, it can slither under a slab of pavement, a pile of leaves, disappear into a crack in a rock wall and be gone.

She practices in the dance studio where she can watch herself in the mirror. A friend of hers, who has a double major in dance and painting, loans her the key. She also helps her refine her moves. The challenge is to be long and thin and very fast. She imagines her body encased in an elastic sleeve, her hands, over her head, the snake's eyes, her torso and tightly pressed together legs and feet, the body and tail. Movement is like swimming on land, except that her limbs can never separate. When her friend comes by, she shows her some traditional Asian dance moves; they give her the kind of fluidity a snake has, curving quickly, elegantly, through the grass.

During the week of presentations, the class meets in the small black-box theater in the performing arts building. Each pair takes the stage, expressing who their partner really is in the allotted ten minutes. She explains that her partner has disappeared, but that they had spent enough time together for her to feel confident in her expression. Her snake slithers convincingly, it lifts its head from the ground like a periscope, watching for any sign of prey, then it pounces in attack, disappearing under a rock with its prey in her mouth, swallowing the animal whole. As soon as she begins, she inhabits Rubiat through the animal, she expresses who he is, and she doesn't care that of all the presentations, hers is the only one that shows cruelty.

The room is quiet. After the other performances there was applause, sometimes laughter, but no one makes a move to congratulate her. At last, a chair creaks as Denton stands up. He walks to the stage. "Thank you," he says in a public voice, and then, softly, "stick around, I want to talk to you."

After the theater empties out, they sit in the front row, side by side, each quarter-turned toward the other. "As you may remember, one of the objectives of this assignment was not to judge. Remember? No flattery, but also, no disapproval. A snake is a potent symbol. Trickery, especially for the female. Think of Eve, the Garden of Eden. Trickery is the *result* of someone's essential nature, it's a consequence, not a quality."

"I used the snake because of its excessive length, its ability to hide."

"But you can't evoke the animal without also evoking the symbol. Just something for you to think about. The snake equals treachery."

"That was not my intention. I chose the snake for its ability to disappear." She can feel her body flaming, knows it gives her away.

She leaves the building quickly. And once she's on her own she realizes he's right. The snake *is* treachery. And if Rubiat had turned on her, then what was his essential emotion? Anger. That is at the heart of treachery.

4

His mother arrives before classes break for the holidays. She meets with his teachers, and then asks to meet with his friends privately. The school gives her a small conference room to conduct the meetings and Rachel's name is on the list, but curiously, in the last slot on the last day. The room is in the basement of the library, down a long, tiled hallway that broadcasts her footsteps. The door is closed and when she knocks a weary voice calls, "Come in!"

The fluorescent lights are off and the figure at the end of the table is shadowed, diminutive. "Come in, Rachel, I certainly appreciate your effort. I know everyone's eager to get home for the holidays."

"Ms. Elsayem, I'm sorry for your loss."

"It's Elsinora. I was never married to Rubiat's father."

"Oh, sorry." The room is charged with the woman's presence; it is the same combativeness Rubiat had, and unable to think of anything else to say, she repeats, "Well, my condolences for your loss."

"Presumed loss. There has been no indication of his death. The boy is simply doing what his father did the year he was born, running away." She has the same angular face as her son, but her coloring is different, blue eyes and a salon-created helmet of blond hair. She is armored in jewelry: rings on her fingers, hoops in her ears, and on her large, maternal breast a necklace of golden, ray-like shapes. Her mouth is the moist color of recently applied lipstick. "I put you on for last because he wrote so much about you in his sketchbook. So I gathered the two of you were close and I hoped you, more than anyone else, could help me locate him."

Rachel crosses her arms over her chest. "I'm sorry, but I didn't know him well at all."

"That surprises me. There are pages and pages. He admired you. He seemed to be studying you and when he drew you, he put on a wash of blue. Captioned it Mother Goodwin."

Rachel laughs. "That was only an assignment. We were partners. I wrote about him too." But then she realizes that she wrote about him after, when she was trying to solve the mystery. He must have written about her before, because they had been together constantly, from the time they were given the assignment to the tragedy, save for the half hour when he went back to his room to drop off his books and change his shoes.

"I heard something about that assignment, but maybe you'd care to elaborate."

"We had to discover each other's essential quality, essential emotion really. That was it, basically. And then express it through movement."

"I see," Ms. Elsinora says. "Odd thing for an art school. This whole place, it seems to me, has an unhealthy, personally invasive tone. I never supported his coming here. And I thought the whole notion of the foundation program was foolish. Shouldn't they be teaching you craftsmanship, materials, skills? How can you become producing artists and make truly exceptional and beautiful things? Instead, it's all this personal exploration, these mind games, these exercises in drama. No wonder he ran away. He must be just as old-fashioned as I am."

Rachel doesn't even attempt to defend. The woman is entitled to her opinion.

"I also heard about your performance. Another student told me, and I find it hugely inappropriate and childish and wonder why you weren't stopped. Maligning another person, comparing them to a poisonous snake. A person who isn't there to defend himself. And especially if you don't know him well. The whole thing seems prurient."

"I assumed he was dead, that's why. Snakes are beautiful creatures. They appear suddenly and disappear just as suddenly. They're strong, they're very definite. And he certainly had those qualities."

"No, he's not dead. He closed his bank account and withdrew everything."

The information rearranges all her assumptions. "When did he do that?"

Ms. Elsinora looks at her sharply, as though this is information she can't give away. But then she seems to change her mind. She lifts an enormous leather folio bag and sets it on the table. The sturdy golden clasp snaps open and she digs through the compartments, pulling out a sheet of paper with the bank's logo. She puts on her glasses. "October 26. He did it in the fifteen minutes before the bank closed for the weekend."

October 27 was the day they went to Stony Brook. It is a date more important than any other date in her life so far, a date when she both gained and lost a lover. He had said he needed to drop off his books, but now it seemed he had also gone to the bank. So, when he found her in the dining hall, he was carrying a bank check in his wallet. When he made love to her, there was a bank check in his wallet in the pocket of the pants he had draped over her chair. And if there were a bank check there, he had made love to her knowing that he was going to leave. "For how much?" she asks.

But this is where his mother draws the line. "I'm not at liberty to say, but it was enough to begin a new life somewhere else. If that's what you're wondering. And although I miss the boy, I have to say I'm relieved this art school nonsense has ended. My family comes from business. They have worked hard, sacrificed everything, and they have been successful because they applied themselves and made intelligent decisions. Running a business, and I know this from personal experience, takes true creativity. And I always thought that was the kind of creativity he possessed."

"What kind of business do you run?" Rachel says. "If you don't mind my asking."

"A shoe store in Manhattan. My grandfather started it as a shoe repair shop. It's very popular, on Ninety-Sixth Street, the Upper West Side. Elsinora Shoes, if you care to know."

"I think he had an accident of some kind. He's dead, I'm sure of it."

"Why would you say that? What did you do, give him drugs?"

"No, I don't do drugs. And Rubiat wouldn't even drink alcohol. I'm sorry, Ms. Elsinora, but I have to get to class."

"Just a few more minutes, please. I've come a long way." She pauses, and then asks, "Why are you so sure he had an accident?"

Rachel doesn't hesitate. "No reason, really. Just a thought." It's a decision she makes quickly, before she has time to question it, and it comes not only from a desire for privacy, but an instinct to hide the chaos of her feelings from his mother.

The woman's glance stays on Rachel's face. She is scared of no one, and as she looks her over, taking her time, making her judgments, there isn't a shadow of sympathy in her hard blue eyes.

"Maybe you wanted him to have an accident. I think you're angry with him. I don't know why, and it's none of my business, but I think there's more than you're telling me. That a school would allow that kind of acting out. Encourage it, even. I have to say, that teacher, Denton Phyfe, did not impress me as a person worthy of guiding young lives. I've looked him up. I know all about him." She taps her pencil on the table, waiting.

But Rachel refuses the bait.

She feels too jangled to go to her next class, so she goes back to the house. She has never lied before and her isolation as the only person who knows the secret truth feels awkward. She rolls the trashcans around to the back, picks up her mail, and slowly climbs the steps to her attic room. Her parents are married, happily it seems, and the only people who've left her life were her mother's parents, residents of Florida who she was never close to. When they died, their absence didn't affect her at all. No one has been sick or moved away, and in her life up until this point, there have been astonishingly few setbacks. Until Rubiat. He took her to a pinnacle of happiness she had

never experienced, and then disappeared. That he had known
he was going to disappear changed everything.

What had he written about her? Had he noticed her disin-
terest? She remembered how, before they were partners, she
wanted nothing to do with him. And then she remembered that
after assigning the project, Denton asked for questions, and
Rubiat, as always, had been the first to respond.

"Isn't it relative how one person sees another? Doesn't it depend on who the observer is and what he or she might want to
see in the other person? I mean, no one is ever really objective,
we're guided by our feelings, our likes and dislikes. I really don't
think you can get around that. People choose to hang out with
the ones who are like them. That's how it always works. I just
think it's going to be a train wreck. Doing something like this."

Denton didn't appear to take offense. Not with Rubiat, not
ever, and Rubiat was always challenging him on one thing or
another. Instead, he said something pretty remarkable, something that helped her certainly and probably all of them. "If
you believe that everything is relative, aren't you destroying the
world of concrete facts? Your hair is dark brown, almost black.
It matches the darkness of your eyes, your heavy eyebrows. You
are tall, not short. These qualities exist. So do other qualities
that are less obvious but also describe you as clearly as the concrete facts I just cited. For instance: You are not timid. You are
not shy. You are punctual. You turn assignments in on time and
you come to class on time and you stay for the whole period.
This is what I'm talking about. Are these essential qualities? I
believe so. Are these your only essential qualities? Maybe, but
someone who interviews you will discover others. You used the
word objective, but I think the duality of objective/subjective
is not relevant for us. A better duality would be concrete and
abstract. That takes us into the world of the artist which is the
world of material things within a context of concept."

The material world. The world of concrete facts: He had
noticed her before Denton paired them. He had closed his
bank account before he met her at the dining hall. He had

changed into rubber-soled shoes. He preferred herbal tea to alcohol. Her mind tiptoed forward: As a lover, he had been patient and attentive. He had helped her achieve orgasm. Those were facts too. But they were private and hers alone. No prying eyes allowed because, for her, it had been the first time she'd experienced that with a partner. Bodies don't lie, and the material world is the world of the body.

That night, as she is falling asleep, she remembers his. The slightly dirty, curly hair. Coarse and springy, thick. The bony shoulders, the muscles in his upper arms, in his chest. There was a line of black hair that ran from nipple to nipple, that grew in a small patch in the center and then, very elegantly, snake-like, sidled down his belly to his groin and there, it was thick and bushy. The penis. She hadn't seen it in a limp state, so she didn't know, really, but erect, it angled off to the side. Very funny. Not circumcised. His buttocks were dimpled in the center, and flat. His thighs strong, muscular. His feet so beautiful. High arches, long toes, neatly clipped toenails. Like his fingernails, which were also clipped. They were flat, not rounded. And though that body might be dead or crippled or wrecked in some way now, it had been hers for one night and half a day. And hers had been his. They had exchanged their bodies, given them to each other to take care of for a short while. And his had given hers such good care until Stony Brook.

She decides not to think about the check. She decides to believe that he had every intention of remaining her partner and doing the assignment and the dive off the cliff had been an impulse, something he had told her he couldn't control.

She knew his body. It had helped her experience the act of love in the deepest way one could, shared and equal. But that was only a first step. Why had he thrown it away?

5

The Spanish Language Institute is on a busy shopping street in Queens, New York. It's a tall, narrow building next to a grocery store that is flanked by stalls of vegetables and fruits. Its pollution-streaked facade blends into the autumn sky. Another autumn. The building doesn't have an elevator, and after climbing four flights, her steps ringing ominously on the metal treads, she comes to a door with a sign, and steps into a waiting room filled with travel posters. She presses a buzzer and a voice hollers from an inner room, "Pase! Come in!"

The room is empty but for a desk and two chairs. A man stands in front of the window, bathed in light. He seems reluctant to turn away from the view. But when he does, he gestures to the chair in front of the desk, and sits down opposite. He is meticulously groomed, the lines of his black goatee etched carefully, a small gold hoop in only one of his earlobes. He looks down at his papers, giving her privacy while she opens her coat and settles herself. She feels too white, too middle class, too distant from her own immigrant history in this teeming, restless neighborhood. It has been decades since anyone in her family has struggled to provide the basic things that people need to survive. She notices how clean his nails are, how white his teeth, how organized his desktop.

"I'm Rachel Goodwin. We spoke on the phone?"

"Ah yes! So you are interested in teaching the beginning class."

"I am, but I have to warn you I don't speak Spanish and I don't have any experience, really, in teaching a language. My years of taking a language, which were in high school, feel very distant."

"Not a problem," he says. "We use the *ABCs of English* textbook and it's very easy for a teacher to follow. Are you familiar with that series, it comes in many languages."

"I'm afraid not."

"Perhaps you can tell me why you are inspired to teach. You must think you'd be good at this, no? Otherwise, why apply?" He leans backward, eyes on her face.

She hesitates. The truth is, she doesn't think she would be good at it.

"I'm listening," he says in a patient tone.

"I don't know. I don't know if I would be good at this or not. I live in the neighborhood and I saw your sign in the supermarket, and I need a job, so I thought I'd ask. That's really the main reason. I need a job."

"You are an unusual applicant, Ms. Goodwin. Most people, including the ones who turn out not to be good at this at all, lie about their qualifications. Or if they don't lie about their qualifications, they lie about the reasons they are excited to teach. It is very unusual to hear someone try to convince me not to hire them. And that makes me quite interested. You see, I am not your usual employer. I began teaching the beginners class and only, as time went on and I understood the need, only then, did I think about creating a place where people could learn in a new way. Immersion, repetition, conversation. It is interesting to me that you choose to tell the truth. Perhaps that will make you a good teacher. You are, clearly, not a good salesperson of yourself. But, who knows, maybe you will be very good as a teacher. Our classes are enormous and they're mostly middle-aged and older people, mostly women. But they want to learn. And it's fairly easy, you see, because you just follow the book. The book teaches them what they need to know and then the class gives them practice in pronunciation and conversing. We pay by the student. The bigger the class, the more you earn. That is your incentive to make the class a welcoming and interesting environment. You see? Look the textbook over, I will loan you a copy, call me in two days either way. Classes are filling and I do need another teacher. And incidentally, contrary to what you may be thinking, your lack of Spanish is a plus. Because if you're fluent, it is tempting to conduct the class in Spanish, which is not our method. We want English immersion. We want the students to be confused, but not too confused, that is, they should be encouraged for their progress, but confusion, a small bit of it, is how they will learn." He gives her a warm smile, pushes a book across the tabletop, and as she walks down the four flights of stairs, she feels as though someone has seen beyond her obvious identity. He has looked past her whiteness and seen something that gives him a glimmer of hope. She will try to believe in that.

Because she is struggling.

After graduation, she tried Rochester for a few months. It seemed like a perfect place to start her adult life. Rents were low, it was easy to find studio space, jobs seemed plentiful, but it was too close to Stony Brook. The mystery of Rubiat's disappearance was a shroud that covered her every moment, blending with the damp weather and perpetual clouds. The other thing that hounded her was the growing feeling that it had been a mistake not to tell anyone what he had done. His act of lunacy was hers alone and it was a burden she didn't know how to carry. The move to New York is her attempt to leave it behind, but if anything, it has been more present. She wants to be done with it, but it's a wound that stays raw.

Queens is the only neighborhood she can afford, and if her parents could see where she is living, their suburban aesthetic would be offended. It's not pretty or appealing in any way. There are no lawns or trees, only electric wires and the unbroken facades of squat buildings. Her studio is in a hulking brick structure that used to be a public school, and her apartment is close to her studio on a quiet street that feels oppressive with tan, nondescript buildings flanked by concrete yards lined with trashcans. On each facade, there is a sign warning against loitering. The shopping streets blare with neon, roar with buses and subways. Sidewalks hold food stalls, small restaurants, enormous, hospital-lit pharmacies, and bodegas with floor-to-

ceiling shelves crammed with necessities, but the bananas, cigarettes, and pastries always in view. Threading her way through
a press of people speaking all languages but English, she has
tried to keep her panic to herself. She is living on pasta, beans,
and coffee, because after the rent, there is nothing left. She
can't afford to take the train into Manhattan; she can't afford
to go to a museum. Friday nights, she splurges on the subway
and goes from one gallery opening to another, looking at art,
dining on free hors d'oeuvres. She needs a source of income,
so she calls, before even looking the book over, and tells him,
yes, she would like to do it. She even lies, says she is excited and
has lots of ideas.

On the day of the first class it rains, and by the evening, it
is raining still. Now that she is an employee, she discovers that
The Language Institute is only five small classrooms and an
office, the name grander than the reality. Metal folding chairs
take over every available space and with umbrellas and rain-
coats dripping on the floor, bodies seating themselves, voices
greeting each other mostly in Spanish, maybe some Portuguese,
she feels like a traitor. They are not individuals, but a multitude
that will determine her paycheck. She writes her name on the
blackboard and points to herself. "I am Rachel." Miming the
act of writing, she asks them to put their names on the piece
of paper she gives to a woman in the front row. That piece of
paper will go to Mr. Pavo after every class; it is the way he will
determine the size of her check. As each person signs, they say
their name out loud, and when the paper comes back to her,
she lays it down on the floor in the corner of the room because
there isn't a desk. "Very good. Now we will describe ourselves."
Pointing to herself she says, "Brown hair, blue eyes, medium
height." She demonstrates short, medium, tall by having people
stand up. Brown eyes are easy to find, as is black hair. They
learn *I am, you are, he, she is* and at the end of the two hours, after
lots of repetition, most everyone can answer simple questions.
The class repeats the words in unison and when she asks individuals what color are their eyes, their hair, they laugh at their

mistakes. *Woman* is a hard sound for them to pronounce; the blocky Germanic sound is inimical to tongues used to softness and flow. She has them repeat it over and over. It is a kind of music, a symphony of voices, and at the end of the first class, she feels as though they are her orchestra, her finger the conductor's baton. She points to the man in the last row. "What is your name?" "My name is José. I am José." A young girl in the middle: "I am Rina. Brown hair, brown eyes. I am tall. She is Consuela. She is tall."

"No, she is not tall."

"I am not tall. I am baja. My name is Consuela."

"Baja?"

The class laughs.

"Short, medium, tall. She is short."

They say it with her: short.

She assigns the first chapter in the book and tells them to do the exercises. At the next class, they want to hand in their answers, but she tells them to write in the book, she won't be collecting assignments. "Class is only for talking. Learning how to talk. We will learn how to talk together." They go over the words they had learned in the first class and progress to naming parts of the body. That is fun. With her baton, she points to her body and they call out the words: arm, leg, chin. Then she says, "What is your best part? The best part is the part you like the most. For instance, I like…" She pauses.

By the second class they are no longer numbers. They are familiar faces, and their voices have already started to populate her lonely life. They are willing and friendly, easy to amuse. Pointing to her chest, she says, "I like my breasts." For a moment they are shocked, speechless. And then one woman begins to laugh, and is soon joined by others, and as they go around the room, it turns out that every woman names her breasts as the best part of her body. There are only two men in the class and one of them says, "I like my hips," demonstrating how they can swivel as he performs a dance move. The other man stands up quickly, shouts out, "I like my hips," singing a tune and swiveling with exaggerated sexual innuendo, miming a partner in his arms.

At the next class there are ten more people, they seem to be friends of the original forty, and when Rachel enters the room, there is a buzz of conversation. There aren't enough chairs, but extra are in the hallway and everyone squeezes closer together to make enough room. They have learned more words from the textbook and now they can say where they are from. I am from Mexico, Columbia, Bolivia. They say the names of their countries in Spanish, but everything else has to be English. The next chapter is on occupation. "My name is Rachel Goodwin and I am from the United States and I am an artist." At their confused looks she adds, "I make things with my hands. Beautiful things. I make boxes with beautiful pictures inside." She says it ten times, very slowly, and asks them, for extra homework, to figure out what she is telling them. They say it back to her: "I make boxes with beautiful pictures inside." Once they figure out what it means, they are to create a sentence to describe what they make that is beautiful.

There are fifty-five at the next class. Chairs take up all the space, leaving barely enough room for her to stand in front of the blackboard. They begin with the sentences they have created, and their eagerness to communicate something important to the others is apparent. "I make beautiful children." "I make beautiful dinner." "I make beautiful dress." "I make beautiful garden." "I make beautiful truck driver."

"What do I do?" she asks them.

"You are artist. You make beautiful boxes!" someone calls out. "You make beautiful boxes with beautiful pictures!" someone else says.

"Where are the beautiful pictures?" Rachel asks.

A young boy, ten, eleven years old, a newcomer to the class, raises his hand and when she calls on him, he says, very carefully, "They are into the boxes." He has come to the class with his abuela and he has a high, chirpy voice and a shy gaze and she hopes his grandmother will bring him again.

6

But she doesn't make boxes. She's never made a box in her life. What she does make are elaborate frames for canvases that, so far, are empty. The frames are the only things that interest her. She decorates them with inlaid wood, and strips of painted, braided canvas. Some have string, ribbons, small bits of embedded metal, and it seems as though, the more elaborate the frame, the more reluctant she is to make a mark on the rectangle of tightly stretched canvas it surrounds. The frames, in and of themselves, are beautiful, and when she walks into her studio and looks at a whole wall of them, some small, some large, they have a presence. The emptiness that is their center feels eloquent and she realizes that when she was inspired to say boxes, she was picturing them as empty, "the beautiful pictures inside" existing only as a phrase of language. Emptiness seems to be the condition that afflicts her. Of course. She is living with a ghost.

On Saturday, she takes the subway into Manhattan. She can afford to do things now; she isn't trapped in Queens. Sometimes she goes into the city without a plan, wandering the streets like a person who has a destination, when it is merely the process of walking and looking that occupies her. It fills her own emptiness, giving her images, sounds, smells she will later, back in her studio, find a way to use in her frames.

This Saturday she takes the subway to the Upper West Side and walks toward the park. It is when she is walking down Seventy-Second Street that she passes a store called The Simple Bag. It is two storefronts, actually, and she can see from the sidewalk that the interior is lined from floor to ceiling with bags of every shape and variety. She gazes in the window at expensive suitcases and valises arranged in a practical, uninteresting manner. There isn't any color, nor are there interesting shapes to attract the eye. The upper reaches of the window are blank, a wasted space that might have been used. When she walks on she is thinking that the store window is a kind of box, a box you can look inside of.

She had expected only to go to the park, but there, on the corner, is the Museum of Natural History. Not of interest, a tomb of bones and rocks, with crowds of frenetic children and loud voices echoing in the marble hallways. She will avoid it.

The leaves have turned red and gold, the sun making halos of the trees in the park, calling her forward. She stays off the populated paths, choosing the smaller, leaf-covered ones, and walks until she gets tired, reliving that other autumn day in the park. By then it is the afternoon and she discovers she has walked in a circle, returning to the same path she had entered on. But it doesn't help; she knows nothing more. From that side of Central Park West, the museum looms importantly, and she realizes it's silly to avoid it. Maybe bones and rocks could tell her something. She climbs the wide steps and enters the grand hall, paying her admission, checking her coat, and wandering wherever she feels inspired to go, skirting the crowds, finding the galleries that aren't popular, the old-fashioned ones, with fake-looking dioramas. It is the dioramas that catch her attention.

In one room there aren't any people at all and instead of large windows that frame scenes with dinosaurs standing against painted backgrounds, models of cacti and stunted trees in a sandy foreground, this room has small windows high in the wall. She looks into one, sees a coiled snake, a rock, a tiny tree, a painted distance of water and sky. She will never be free of it. She will never know what really happened. She will never be able to leave the airless room of their secret. She feels it when she returns to her studio. The empty canvases hanging on the wall, elaborate frames holding nothing. Something essential is gone from her life. Where is he? *Is* he? Is *she*?

That's the question. She doesn't seem to *be* any longer, as though when he dove off the cliff, he took her with him. That's why it was so easy to lie. They were both gone. That's why she can't paint, but only frame. She is missing as much as he is. Box. Maybe it's a clue from her unconscious. "I make boxes with beautiful pictures inside." Those words, uttered in class without thinking, were instructions. Her soul was instructing her. She must abandon the frames and create a box to hold that October day, to give it a place, to finish it. She finds a lumberyard and buys thin sheets of plywood, and that afternoon, they deliver them to her studio.

Unfinished. In process. In class she introduces gerunds. Building, singing, speaking. Active verbs are easy to demonstrate. Each person mimes an action and she supplies the word. "You are hopping. You are turning. I am laughing."

But what is she doing? She is living in New York, going to shows and museums, getting to know the gallery world, and feeling hopeless and confused about her life as an artist. She is afraid the box will only be another dead end. Meanwhile, she is surrounded by people, on the subway, in her neighborhood, in her building, the rapid Spanish in the hallway outside her apartment. Qué pasa? No pasa nada. Her class has maxed out at fifty-five and is holding. She makes enough money to buy a piece of fish, and every once in a while, go to a movie. Sometimes she goes with Angela, her one friend. Angela went to school with her and graduated a year before. She is Chinese American, works in a dumpling shop, and lives in an apartment with her grandmother. She has a huge extended family, friends from childhood, but no one, besides Rachel, who understands her life as an artist.

"What if I come over tonight? Is that good? I'll bring dumplings, okay? Like, around seven?"

This is how Angela summons her. It is always spontaneous, always with dumplings. She likes to come to Rachel's apartment because Chinatown is stuffy and provincial; there are too many relatives. She needs the fresh air of Rachel's Spanish neighborhood. When Rachel first moved into her apartment, Angela presented her with chopsticks and a bamboo steamer, warning her that it was a selfish gift because they were going to have a lot of dinners together. Angela always brings dumplings from the shop where she works. The plump pillows of white dough filled with chopped vegetables and meat or fish are a blend of delicate flavors Rachel craves. In Angela's company, she regains her old confidence. She cleans her tiny space, knowing how meticulous Angela is, and buys greens for a salad and a six-pack of beer. Angela inspires her. She is articulate and beautiful and makes small paintings out of intricate geometric designs that buzz and pulse with restless colors. Rachel dusts her shelves, cleans off her stovetop, and has just swept the floor when her buzzer chimes.

She opens the door, listening to the distant footfalls as her friend climbs the many flights, rounding all the turns in the echoing hallways of her building and then she arrives, her bubbling, jubilant energy filling the tiny hallway. She sets her packages on the counter and Rachel unwraps the dumplings and layers them in the steamer. They move to the living room, but Angela is restless. She wanders through the rooms, taking long sips of her beer. "I had to let two trains go by they were so crowded. I am so ready for this! The special today was pork so there's lots of pork, but there's also something you haven't had before. It's new. You'll be amazed. Soup dumplings! How are you?"

This is what Rachel loves about her. They are the same height, have the same slender bodies, but Angela is a cultural crossroads: traditional Chinese, contemporary American, identities that are uneasy with each other. Where the unease evaporates is here, in Rachel's apartment, the place where a third identity is the only thing that matters, the artist, that is, the one who mixes things up, who lives by intuition and feeling, who is impractical, arbitrary, and tirelessly demanding. Nurtured in art school, the artist demands time and focus, and they are both committed to doing her bidding.

Rachel sits at the opposite end of her small couch, facing Angela. "I'm stuck. I keep on making frames around blank canvases. And what I realized today, well, I went to the Natural History Museum, and do you know what I discovered? Dioramas. You know, those lit spaces that illustrate different kinds of environments? The viewer looks through a window at a scene that seems totally realistic? There's something about that, it's like your own private theater. Of course, at the museum, they're pretty hokey. I mean, *very* hokey. But what if you weren't even *trying* to make something that was realistic. What if you peered through a small window at pattern and color and…I don't know. What if you peered through a small window and you saw a painted door, but it's open a little bit, and there's a glimpse of something behind it, and behind that, another opening of some kind, so it's viewing an ever-increasing distance with only hints of the end point, which is either radiance or darkness, I don't know. Look at my arm! I have goosebumps. Just talking about it, I feel this shivery sensation."

"There's a ghost in the room. That's what my grandmother always says. You're feeling a ghost. I think they're ready. Don't they smell ready?"

Angela comes back from the kitchen with a bamboo basket on a plate. Rachel lights two candles and they sit at her small table.

"Do you remember those Joseph Cornell boxes? I remember that you didn't like them."

"You do? How do you remember that?" Rachel hadn't liked the interiors that Joseph Cornell had created inside of boxes, using found objects that he rearranged in intriguing ways.

"You were kind of opinionated about it. Wouldn't shut up about it, as I recall."

"I guess I was. I found them too flat, too loaded with significance. I want to stay away from meaning and symbolism. I want to simply deliver experience. Look, there goes my arm again." She holds up her arm and there, again, are goosebumps, her delicate blond hairs lifting up in response to a vibration she can't feel.

"Who is it? That's what's important."

Rachel knows Angela believes in the occult. It's on display everywhere in Chinatown, the many shops with potions and herbs, the storefronts that have been turned into spaces for prayer with golden fabrics and decorated altars. "I don't know. Everyone in my family's still alive. Everyone who matters, that is. I never really knew the grandparents who died."

"This is a soup dumpling," Angela says, holding a fat, squirmy pillow between two chopsticks. "Bite into it, you'll see."

Rachel takes the soft dough into her mouth and feels the delicious broth explode on her tongue. "Amazing! How do you ever make those?"

"Practice, but I'm very good at it now."

Once, when she was downtown, Rachel stopped by the dumpling shop; customers could look through the window on the street and see the cook working at a table in the back of the store. In a crisp white apron, Angela faced the window, but kept her eyes on her job as she filled and wrapped, filled and wrapped, fingers flying. Rachel was reluctant to tap at the window and break her focus, so she simply walked on.

"You never told me what happened back then," Angela says. "With Rubiat. Did he die?"

"His mother didn't think so. But, Angela, that was three years ago. I hardly remember him." As Rachel speaks, she realizes that lies feel like truth if you say them out loud. "He was a strange guy. We had a one-night stand and then he died or disappeared, who knows."

"Was it memorable?"

She feels a tightening in her chest. This is her good friend. "It was. The best ever." Her cheeks color, but in candlelight she knows Angela can't see.

"I didn't know if there had been anything between you guys. By the way, I want you to meet someone. He's an old friend and he's not Chinese."

Rachel interrupts to say, "That wouldn't be a problem!"

"Well, he moved to the city recently, but I know him from this art camp I went to in high school. He's a good guy, I think you would like him."

"I'm perfectly happy the way things are. I don't mind being lonely, so don't feel you have to."

"I know, and I don't. Look, why not meet him as a friend? Expand! Reach out! I'll cook a dinner and have you both over. And Grandma will be there, but she goes to bed early."

"What does he do?"

"He works at a food co-op. But he's also a musician. That's what he really cares about."

She wishes she had gone back once again, just to investigate. Even though she'd taken the police to the spot on the upper trail and they had searched the lower trail, both sides, and no one saw any signs of him, maybe what seemed to be a solid face of shale had a hidden crevice, or a shelf big enough to fit a body. And maybe the helicopter hadn't seen it, maybe the pilot was distracted, maybe he was looking at the wrong places. The green pants. They could have blended in and kept him hidden. Because a person could not simply become a ghost. Despite what Chinese grandmothers believed.

7

Dusty knows he can't survive in the city. He has different needs than other people and he blames it on his country childhood. He needs to see the reflection of sunlight on a brook edged in winter ice, the russet flash of a fox streaking through a meadow of sapling trees. He likes harvesting wood, growing vegetables, keeping a cow, raising chickens. He even likes hunting deer though he isn't sure that would square with Buddhist practice. But despite these things, he lives in Brooklyn, New York, far away from foxes, deer, and stands of harvestable trees.

He lives in a dharma house. He meditates every day, sitting on a low red cushion in the altar room, a small room off the hallway on the second floor where there is a figure of the seated Buddha on a low table with bowls of offerings. He has a rope of beads on which he counts his prayers and like everyone else in the house (Shelby, Aaron, Hazel) he wears his beads around his neck, but tucked out of sight under his shirt.

Sometimes, when he sits in front of the Buddha, he goes into a meditative trance and as stillness floods his chest, all the trivialities of his life feel far away. He can walk himself into the same trance when he wanders through the park that is close to the dharma house and the vision of trees and space fills his senses. He can feel the minds of the trees, bushes, even the stones, and he can walk, aimless and entranced, for a long time. There are private areas in Prospect Park, pathways through the woods, or corners of hidden lawn, and he has noticed other entranced people standing still or sitting quietly, their attention caught. Of course, maybe they're waiting for sex or drugs, but he doesn't think so. He can tell by the quiet around their bodies that they too are entranced, that they're feeling the embrace of the air, the flash of birds, the shapes of branches and pathways, the tangle and order of the life around them.

Sometimes he'll be walking along a path and see a tree standing by itself in a field and is overwhelmed by its solitary presence, and walking up to touch it and thank it for its existence is necessary, but hardly enough. Each day, walking by, he bows his head and renews his thanks.

The walk through the park is the most efficient way to get to his job at the co-op and those minutes of solitude and gratitude, passing through a green, breathing space in the midst of a dense neighborhood, helps prepare him for the onslaught of demands that will overtake his oxygenated body as soon as he crosses the threshold into the store.

They need him because he understands the food chain better than city people. He understands eggs from free-range chickens, milk from grass-fed cows, meat from animals that have never been exposed to the sad conditions of a feedlot. Those aren't just labels. They mean specific things. The others don't grasp that. When he'd intervened in the eggs, for instance, he had to tell them that if the yolk isn't an intense yellow, then that chicken was not outside eating bugs and grass. And when he'd tested it, finding pale yolks in cartons of eggs claiming to be all the buzz words people liked, he'd stopped using those suppliers. He had to explain it to them. They thought the words meant something, in and of themselves, but they were simply advertising. "If a chicken is eating grass and leaves and insects, its eggs will have a bright orange yolk in the summer, a bright yellow yolk in winter. If it's raised inside a building and has a diet only of commercial chicken feed, even if it's organic, the yolk will be a pale color."

They need his experience, these city people. For instance, some green leafy vegetables, kale and collards for instance, became sweeter after a frost, so they should stick with local suppliers through the winter, not have it shipped from the big organic enterprises in California. Hell, when he was a kid, they'd brush the snow off the kale patch, cut the frozen stalks, and bring them into the house to thaw for dinner. They promoted him to buyer. That is a huge responsibility. Fifty thousand dollars every week on eggs and vegetables. The Parkside Food Co-op is the largest food buyer in all of Brooklyn, bigger even than Whole Foods. And it has history. It's the oldest non-profit, member-run food cooperative in the entire United States. He is proud to be a part of it and happy with his new life. All the puzzle pieces fit miraculously and though Brooklyn is a city, Dusty Lenox is surviving very well. An old friend is just a subway ride away and he thinks maybe something with her can happen. He'd called her as soon as he had arrived, and they'd met a couple of times for coffee. It had been friendly, maybe even more than friendly. She's Chinese American and the cultural gap sometimes makes it difficult to read her intentions.

8

Rachel speaks to her brother every few weeks. Though they're only two years apart in age, they were never friends in childhood, becoming close only during the year after college when she tried life in Rochester. His name is Edward, it's not Eddie or Ed, as he always makes clear, and he's almost a dentist, almost finished with his schooling. He's also almost married. They don't live together, but Ann, Edward's girlfriend of six years, is a constant in his life.

But that's not what they talk about. The subject they share confidences on is sex. For each, they have become the representative of the opposite gender, giving advice, offering opinions. This role became clear when Rachel decided that Rochester couldn't work. Edward made dinner for her, he's an excellent cook, and Ann also joined them. She arrived with an apple pie.

It was over dessert that the questions began. Ann served the pie. It was from scratch, she was famous for her flaky crusts, and as she hefted the still warm pieces, filling tumbling out, breasts straining the buttons of her blouse, apple falling from the spatula, because Edward didn't have a proper pie server, her cheeks were flushed with wine, her light hair was spilling about her face, and Rachel felt as though she were seeing a color plate from an art history book, a painting by Rubens, translated to a modern house. Then she noticed that Edward was not part of it. He was still in the kitchen, fiddling with the coffee. Ann was apologetic because the pie had fallen apart. "It's too warm; I'm so sorry; I was too rushed. I should have started it earlier so it had enough time to cool."

But Rachel didn't care. And no matter how many times she said it didn't matter, that it was going to be delicious, Ann didn't listen. Nothing would persuade her to forgive herself. No wonder Edward stayed in the kitchen, she thought. She would have stayed in the kitchen too.

Coffee served, pie eaten, and it *was* delicious, though maybe a bit too sweet, Edward said, "You know, I wish you could stay. I wish you could make it work. Rochester is so much more affordable than New York and it's wonderful having you here."

"For me too. I wish it could have worked, but…well, something happened and it's cast this pall over everything and I realized that if I'm going to be productive I have to leave this city."

"What happened?" Edward asked.

"Edward!" Ann interjected. "She would tell us if she wanted to. Right, Rachel?"

"Thanks, Ann, and I would. It's just hard to talk about and really private."

"Were you raped or something?"

"Well, no, I wasn't raped. But someone betrayed me in a startling kind of way, and I don't think I've gotten over it. It happened at school, two years ago, so it's been a while, and I think what I need is a change in scenery."

Later, on the phone, when Edward called to say goodbye, he asked about it again, and she realized that she could tell him alone, she hadn't wanted to also tell Ann and then have Ann leak it to their parents. She knew she could trust Edward to keep it to himself.

"A man I fell in love with killed himself in front of my eyes. It was at Stony Brook. He jumped off a cliff."

"Oh God," he breathed, and she could feel his concern. "I'm so sorry, Rachel. That's awful and now I totally understand."

"Just keep it to yourself, okay? Not even Ann."

"Don't worry," and in the way he quickly assured her she knew he understood why Ann couldn't be privy to it. And in a way, that was how their absolute trust in one another began.

"If I'm so in love with Ann, why am I attracted to Ruby?"

Edward has called her one evening, and after discussing their parents' upcoming anniversary party, he tells her about a fellow student.

"Are you?"

"What, in love or attracted?"

"In love."

He chuckled. "Of course I am. Why do you ask?"

"Sometimes you seem… Never mind, just tell me what attracts you to this other woman."

"She's sultry, steamy, she exudes something that feels like a complete openness to passion."

"Can you describe her?"

"I dream about her enough, so let's see. Olive skin, dark hair, very thin, almost angular and boyish. Why am I attracted when I have this curvy goddess?"

"Because you are," Rachel tells him. "And you owe it to yourself to find out what that's about."

"I don't even know if she's interested."

"Come on, Edward, of course she is. As another woman, I'm telling you, you can be certain of that." Her brother doesn't look like Rachel. He has the dusky complexion and dark hair of the Spanish ancestor their mother's family, the Normals of Ohio, hid among their mostly English forebears. As a child, Edward looked so 'other,' people might have wondered if he had been adopted, or who, really, his father was. But any suspicions would have been quickly squashed by the protective bond the Goodwin parents created between them, a bond that allowed no critics or detractors and was part of the reason they pressured Rachel to settle down in Rochester.

"I've known her for a long time and we've always been friendly but when she sits next to me, I feel this sensation, you know, this electricity."

"I do know," Rachel says, happy to speak from experience.

"And I wonder if she looks at me too long."

"When she was looking at you, what was she wearing?"

"She looks really beautiful in black. All black, that's what she usually wears."

"Ask her out. What can she do, refuse?"

"And what do I tell Ann?"

"Don't," Rachel says. "Don't tell her a thing."

"You don't like her, do you?"

"Of course I like her, but I also don't want you to feel trapped and Ann is just like us. Maybe you need someone who's different."

"How do you know Ruby's different? You've never met her."

She notices the closeness of their names, Ruby, Rubiat, and files it away. And then she realizes that Edward is the different one too, though she still thinks of their family group as pale and blue-eyed. "I can tell from the excitement in your voice. Your...I don't know, I can hear this pleasure. I would see it on your face, Edward, I'm sure you have a gleam in your eyes. I can hear it."

"But maybe that's just the excitement of someone new, someone different."

"Exactly. And that's what you should pay attention to."

9

Angela learned how to cook by watching her grandmother. Chopping, slicing, shredding, mincing, wielding a heavy cleaver with fast, practiced precision, her grandmother would prepare piles of vegetables to mix with trimmed, sliced meat or fish. She'd drip oil into the wok, shake to distribute an even slick, and then, one by one, would cook each pile according to the length of time it needed, longer cooking things going in first. She didn't approve of the gray mushiness of American food and cooked on very high heat to retain color and crunch, filling the kitchen with the aroma of herbs and spices, always the first things she added to the oil.

She'd shake and stir constantly, waiting until the contents reached a harmonious balance of color, texture, and fragrance. Then the wok was turned over a platter, its contents nudged out with a wooden spoon. Rice was scooped from an electric cooker. Cups of tea, a tea pot filled with more on the sideboard. This was how Angela was raised. The meals, cooked quickly, were consumed slowly, white plastic chopsticks flashing.

She and her grandmother choose the menu for Angela's friends. Sesame noodles, five spice tofu, Buddha's garden, hot pepper green beans. Dusty didn't eat meat or fish but he did eat animal products that were given freely, so when the broth is boiling, she whisks in beaten egg, adds a finely chopped chili for a hint of hot.

She and her grandmother work side by side, hardly speaking, the small kitchen fragrant with steam. Angela has purchased a pint of green tea ice cream for dessert and hides it in the back of their freezer because her grandmother doesn't approve of dessert. Intense sweet at the end of the meal wipes out the balance of taste the cook has worked so hard to attain. But she'd be in bed by then.

She had warned everyone to come on time so they could meet her grandmother before she retired to her room and the first person who rings the bell is Dietrich. She opens the window, throws down the key. Tied to a red enamel soup spoon that slows its descent from six stories to the sidewalk below, it's easy to see. Soon, his tread on the stairway is apparent.

Dietrich is a rosy-cheeked, blond German. Broad shoulders, a round ass that she has yet to see without clothes, he is like candy, sweet to her salt, a confection she is proud to show off to Lin Lin who disapproves of Chinese men who have been converted to the American religion, shiny addictions and absence of faith, like her husband, but not her son, Angela's father. Dietrich had come to the shop. He was from the newspaper and was doing a story on Chinese dumplings. She invited him back when the shop closed and it was then, heads bent together over the single table, language swirling, questions, answers, names of ingredients, she'd felt the spark. Her grandmother invites Dietrich into the living room, gestures to the bench that serves as a sofa, and says, "Please. To drink? Beer, soda, tea, wine?"

"Wine would be grand," Dietrich says. He has brought in the cold air, and as Angela carries his coat to the closet, she feels its heft and respectability, noticing the silk lining, the elegant, embroidered label.

By the time all three of the guests have arrived, and the red spoon is back on the hook by the door, the tiny apartment is overflowing with voices. Lin Lin has met everyone, brought each the beverage of choice, and then, with bowed head, clasped hands, wishes them a good evening. She shuffles back to her bedroom with her sedative, a tea she's brewed from mushrooms and barley, balanced on a sturdy plastic tray. The door to her bedroom closes and the four are alone.

Angela has never brought foreigners to her apartment before, and as she takes in these three very different friends she loses courage. What in the world could an artist, a journalist, a co-op manager, and a dumpling maker find to talk about? Her grandmother had been so natural with them, so welcoming, but she is old-fashioned, and her age keeps the lines of communication strict. But as a Chinese granddaughter and American contemporary, she is pulled in two directions at once. This is the reason she has always kept her home life private. But now that they are here, and the fortress has been breached, maybe the first thing is to be a traditional Chinese host and welcome them.

"I am so happy you've come. This is Lin Lin's apartment. She is my dearly beloved grandmother and friend. She's the one who taught me how to be. More than my parents. And when she turned eighty-seven, three years ago, just when I was getting out of school, she asked me to live with her. Though not exactly like that. She said, I am an old woman and of no use to anybody anymore, but perhaps I can offer you a place to live and a last friendship before I am summoned. I would like that very much if you would like it too."

"She said that in Chinese?"

"Yes, Mandarin. She doesn't speak much English. She never has to, living here."

"She's so elegant, so kind. She really seems wonderful. And how amazing to offer you a place to live."

"I work just a few blocks away. And we know everyone in the building. Everyone's Chinese."

"It's like my town in Bavaria," Dietrich says. And then he describes the extended family there, the old farmhouse, the pastures where they have grazed sheep for decades.

Dusty talks about his hippie parents, their life of self-subsistence, heating with wood, growing their food, raising chickens. His father had built their cabin himself. At first it was a small, dark place, but when his brother and sisters were born, he built an addition. They had electricity and running water, but they heated and cooked with wood and harvested all the wood themselves by thinning their forests.

"There's nothing exotic about me," Rachel says. "I come from the suburbs of a cold, snowy city and my parents have ordinary middle-class lives. I'm your typical American, kind of boring."

"That must be why you came here," Dusty says.

"What do you mean?"

"To this enormous, chaotic city."

"I came really for the galleries and museums and the art community. And Angela was here. That was definitely a draw. But I guess I was escaping."

"I am escaping as well," Dietrich says.

"I'm definitely escaping," Dusty says. "My parents' life is too hard. They have no money and I don't know what's going to happen to them in twenty years. How are they going to cut wood and grow vegetables? Who's going to take care of them? I mean, just cooking on a wood cookstove, it takes a huge amount of wood split down to small diameters."

Angela watches in amazement as everyone finds this common ground and by the time she puts the food out on the table in the kitchen, these three people who were strangers just an hour before are talking excitedly and her Bavarian confection has taken off his sweater and vest (the kitchen is very hot) and rolled up his sleeves.

The food has been warming in the oven (her grandmother had placed a pan of steaming water on the bottom shelf to keep things moist) and now she begins with soup.

"Oh, egg drop, that's my favorite."

"Just a little spicy, how perfect."

And then, moving on to the rest, she watches these friends. Was her confection a friend yet? He is a good eater. She had worried he wouldn't know how to use chopsticks and the only forks her grandmother has are big ones for serving, but he is as adept as everyone else. His mustache glistens with the oils of her labors and she knows they will get along. Now, others remove their sweaters, roll up sleeves, shuck off scarves and by the time she brings out the green tea ice cream there are murmurs of protest. She suggests they move back to the living room where she opens a window to let in a scoop of cold air. Then she pours cups of her grandmother's mushroom barley tea and serves the ice cream in tiny blue and white bowls. Dietrich is a man of good appetite. Her grandmother would approve. And Dusty and Rachel seem to have connected. Rachel has a long trip back to Queens and she makes sure Dusty leaves with her.

When the door shuts behind them, she turns to Dietrich and says, "Would you like a little more ice cream, tea, wine?"

He takes a little of everything and that is when she knows he will do very well. This is how her grandmother had met her grandfather. She'd cooked for him, but when they came to this country, he became hollowed out, worthless for anything but playing mahjong with his drinking pals. There is no danger of hollow with Dietrich.

10

He realizes, as soon as he gets to her apartment and meets Rachel and Dietrich that it is a setup. Angela is the game master, moving the pieces around the board. Two women, two men, and it isn't clear to him, at first, what the hostess's intentions might be.

He meets the tiny grandmother. She hands him a glass of plum wine, sweet and viscous, in a small, fluted goblet. There is a spray of pussy willow in a highly glazed ceramic vase painted with cherry blossoms. That is in a corner of the living room which probably hasn't had a fresh coat of paint in thirty years.

Everywhere he looks are objects from a distant past. The couch is from the fifties, sleek but worn, and even the grandmother's deference toward them feels old-fashioned and out of place. Another side of Angela, something he has never considered. Nothing of hers is on view anywhere. Cheap Chinese scrolls, the kind you see in tourist shops, decorate the walls. Yet she could live here and she is happy, you can tell. The whole neighborhood, it is a small Chinese village. Seeing it now, realizing this is what had formed her, he thinks she is more beautiful than ever and he feels impatient with the others. Why are they here? Inviting him was a kind of pulling back of the curtain, an undressing of her whole self, and maybe she's invited the others just so it isn't so obvious.

At first, he thinks Dietrich and Rachel have come together. They have the same healthy red cheeks, the same Germanic solidity. But he mustn't make assumptions. These days one has to be careful, and as soon as Rachel opens her mouth, he knows she is American. Dietrich is busy revving up the Aryan accent because women always find a foreigner more appealing. Which leaves him the odd man out. But he won't retreat. He'll just have to work a little harder.

Dietrich is serious competition. He has the social poise of a man who earns his living by connecting with people. Angela, for instance. He interviewed her for an article, not yet published, called "The Secrets of Chinese Dumplings." Dusty tells him about the co-op, that it is the oldest in the country, etcetera, etcetera, but he can tell the man has no real interest and is only being polite. And being European how would he know about the whole hippie movement anyway, when food co-ops were everywhere? It comes to him suddenly that Rachel is not with Dietrich. She is a friend of Angela's from art school and it is also clear that Angela has invited her for Dietrich. Well, it will be interesting to watch play out. They look so much alike they could be siblings.

The women Dusty is attracted to have something exotic, or odd, or unique about them. He can be friends with sensible, hard-working females, but it takes a glimpse of something unusual to awaken his libido. Maybe it's the meditation. It keeps him too even or something, too satisfied, too unneedy.

The food is amazing. They eat in the kitchen at a small table, one person on each side, knees and elbows touching. Luckily, there is a good red wine, courtesy of Dietrich, and the plum stuff disappears. He has seconds of everything, wanting to draw the dinner out, waiting for a signal from Angela that he should stay on, but when Rachel says it's time she headed out, Angela brings his coat too. "You're both going to the same station, might as well go together." It's a slap in the face, stunning for the way it comes out of nowhere, toppling his assumptions.

They walk toward Canal Street. The night is still and cold and to his surprise, they talk easily. When they pass a café, she suggests they duck inside for a cup of tea and, still feeling Angela's rejection, he agrees. But as they sit down at a filthy table no one is in a hurry to clear, he wonders why he is doing this. She is so squeaky clean, so American, so white and provincial. She tells him about her English as a second language classes, how eager the people are, how crowded the little room.

"You must be a good teacher," he says.

That is when she leans forward and in a low voice (the place is empty and the guy at the counter is obviously listening), she says, "There's something very strange that happens. It happens every time. I feel like I'm making music, like I'm conducting an orchestra of voices. It's very odd. I want to give as many people as possible a chance to talk, so I call on them to say something in English. They speak these very basic sentences slowly. *My dress is red. My scarf is here. The woman is tall.* All these different voices, their tones, rhythms, their different accents. It's music. I think they feel it too, because they get very animated. They speak loudly and with conviction even though they make mistakes. Like last week someone said, 'I am happy to sleep.' And someone else said, 'I am happy to pay.' Or no, it was, 'I am happy to not pay.' And then, 'I am happy to grow old,' and someone else said, 'I am not happy to grow old.' I've never written music, I've never played an instrument, but it feels so musical. What if someone were to come in with a guitar, say, or a keyboard and we see what would happen? I think it would be pretty exciting."

"I play guitar," Dusty says. It sounds like he is volunteering and he isn't sure he wants to do that.

"Really? What kind of music?"

"The old stuff. The folk songs. Things I grew up with. My hippie parents, you know. But I love that stuff. James Taylor, Judy Collins, Joan Baez. It's really dated, I know, but those are the songs I love. My parents loved them and they passed it onto me."

It tumbles out so quickly and suddenly they are making plans for Dusty to come to the last class of the semester. How did that happen? She is saying thank you, good to meet you, etcetera, etcetera. He mouths appropriate words back, and then they each go to their different tracks in the sprawling underground station.

11

When the day arrives, she is nervous. She has such a good rapport with the students, maybe it's foolish to bring in a new person.

She told them about their visitor the week before. "We will be making music," she said. "We will be singing and talking to music." That evening, before her announcement, they had reviewed the verb, to feel, and how it could be paired with adjectives: *I feel sad, he feels sad, you feel happy*. Then she introduced the words *music, song, instrument, conductor*, all of which were in a chapter of their book called *Sounds*.

For *song*, she sang a song. This caused them to laugh. She had a passable voice, nothing remarkable, but she sort of pulled it off. *Conductor* was an easy one to mime, and for instrument, she taught them guitar, miming a person playing it. "Guitarra!" someone called out and she said, "Yes! At our last class we will—notice the future tense, will—make music." She wrote some sentences on the board and for homework they were to answer them: Do you sing? Do you play an instrument? Do you like music?

When she comes up the stairs she hears excited voices and opens the door to find there are even more people. The grandmother who came with her grandson has also brought her daughter. Someone has set up a card table and there are snacks and drinks. Someone has brought cookies, others have brought wine and beer. She hadn't intended an actual party, but they are excited and she realizes there is nothing wrong with it. The building is empty, there aren't any classes after theirs, and who would know? Dusty is late, so she begins with the homework questions. It turns out that those who play instruments have brought them to class. "I play horn," a tall man says, and opens a case to reveal a trumpet. "I play guitar," a teenager says, and he plugs it in and strums a few notes. The grandmother stands up with her daughter and grandson and in unison they say, "We sing." A pregnant woman who always spoke softly declaims, in a loud voice, "I like music. My husband like music, my son like music."

That is when they hear footsteps coming down the hallway. Dusty waits at the door until she beckons him forward and presents him to the class. "My friend. He plays guitar and he sings." As Dusty takes off his coat and pulls his guitar out of the case, she writes his name on the board and they practice saying it. He pulls a chair to the front of the room and sits down, tuning. The horn player joins him at the front and then beckons the other guitar player to come forward. Dusty plays a simple tune and the others join in, and soon they are in unison. She teaches them the words *trumpet* and *electric guitar*. Then she stands next to the musicians and says, "When I point to you, say or sing any sentence you'd like." She points to the pregnant woman who sings, "I like music." She has a surprisingly clear voice and follows the melody. The next person sings, "I like music," and as she moves from person to person, each one sings, "I like music," all of them attempting to follow the tune. The grandmother stands up with her children and they sing in harmony, "I like music," in clear, beautiful voices and as others in the room say their sentence, the three of them harmonize in the background. The trumpet and electric guitar become emboldened and at the height of things, a man stands up with a harmonica he pulls from his pocket and joins the musicians. It goes on and on. She no longer has to point, people simply sing whatever sentence they like, one person singing, "I like the teacher," others joining in and then the grandmother changing it to "I like Rachel," her trio singing it loudly. Rachel steps into the middle of this euphoric fest, and harmonizing as best as she can, sings, "I like my students."

She invites him back to her apartment.

"I like Rachel," he whispers before tumbling out of bed when the alarm sounds in the morning. It will take him an hour to get to his house from her apartment in Queens and this is the third morning he's done it. He stops at his house to take a shower, change clothes, eat something, and then heads out for the co-op, going through the park.

He has never been this kind of person before, someone who is always rushing, who stumbles onto the subway barely awake, hoping for a seat so he can sip the hot coffee he's purchased from a cart. He's never been so normal. Usually, his days started with an hour of meditation, but Rachel has changed all of that. She has offered to stay over at his house for a night or two, but he isn't sure he wants to bring home someone he doesn't feel totally committed to. It's just sex, nothing deep or life changing. She isn't Buddhist, and that's another reason. She wouldn't understand the beads, the altar room, the thangkas hanging on the walls. It's like a seminary, and she just wouldn't get it.

But most of all, he likes her place. The bright red rug, the bright blue cushions on an otherwise drab sofa that looked secondhand. The things on the wall, collages of torn paper in interesting shapes. He likes slipping out of her room without waking her, kissing her warm neck before shutting the door and entering the streets full of people on the move. Like he has a high wage job in finance or medicine, and not a job at a co-op. He likes being part of the crowds rushing from train to train while inside, in his private world, he is still touching her body. He has discovered the things she likes. He knows the ways to get her excited and he plays her expertly, just as she, after a time, has learned to play him.

Of course the first time was awkward, but everything is working now and still, there are surprises. The music changes and soon, in the third month, he has stopped seeing her on weeknights. The excitement of the commute wore off quickly and he wants to get back to his Buddhist practice, so they have switched to weekends only. They eat dinner out, Queens has cheaper, better restaurants, and when they get back to her apartment he often plays for her. They don't talk much, but maybe that's because things between them have slipped into a comfortable groove. They don't need to talk, certainly not about the relationship.

Of course, no one has mentioned love. It seems beside the point. Good sex: that's as far as they go for now.

12

I t's January, a year later, when he receives the call from a
co-op in Philadelphia. He's been recommended by one of
their suppliers as someone who understands the challenges
and concerns of cooperatives, who knows both the market and
the supply side, and they want him to apply for a position that
has just opened up. He fills out their form and sends it in and
doesn't give it another thought. Two weeks later they call to set
up an interview. He doesn't bring any of this up with Rachel
because he has no desire to move and is going through the
motions only so he can ask for an increase in salary. The Philadelphia job not only pays better but has better benefits.

He takes the train down. Two people pick him up at the station, take him out to lunch to talk about the job, and the more
he hears, the less he's interested. It's a neighborhood store with
a small membership and a small shopping space. They drive
him to an area of the city called Germantown and park in front
of a commercial building on a block of stores shaded by elm
trees that are so tall and healthy it seems they haven't heard of
the disease that felled their brethren. But that is only the first
of many surprises.

The store is clean, orderly, well-stocked, and unlike the co-
op in Brooklyn, the ratio of membership to shopping space
is reasonable. Shelves and bins are restocked not five times a
day, but only once. In the basement storage area there is one
refrigerated room, not two. Delivery trucks pull around to the
loading dock in the back of the building, not on a busy street
in the midst of traffic where unloading happens on the sidewalk. They come one at a time on a weekly, rather than a daily
schedule. Only three members work a time slot, not twenty,
and yet there are five full-time staff, just as in Brooklyn. He
would be the man in charge. Working days would be relaxed,

not frenzied, and he would set the tone and pace. He would be the voice of the organization. He asks about rents and their answers are another surprise. After the interview, they drive him around Germantown. There are big, old houses with deep front porches, large yards, and tall trees. Here and there, he can see the remains of summer vegetable gardens. Then they take him to the train station and he tells them he's very impressed, very interested.

He could have a life here. Surely there is a Buddhist center in Philadelphia. He'd have to buy a car, of course, but Germantown is a place you could easily walk to a restaurant, a hardware store, go out for a drink. He could live in walking distance of the co-op. The houses are so large, Rachel could have a studio at home. She wouldn't have to teach. She could paint full time, and best of all, she would be close enough to New York to visit galleries and museums.

He notices the drift of his thoughts. Yes, it is premature, but what is wrong with thinking ahead? Nothing is a sure thing until he signs a contract.

That week, he spends his evenings on the internet learning about this city that is only two hours south of New York. There *is* a Buddhist center, and the Philadelphia Museum is world class. That should interest Rachel. The area called Germantown is even older than it looks and in those sprawling brick and stone houses there are apartments with square footage that is unheard of in Brooklyn. And yet, compared to New York, they're affordable. They could have a dog. That's the other thing about Germantown. It's on the edge of an enormous park where he could walk the dog every morning. They would get a mutt, not a breed. They would go to the shelter and give a caged animal a good life. He pictures himself standing on the porch of a stone house with a dog pulling at the leash, straining toward the sidewalk. There he is, walking the dog toward the park, passing one beautiful house after another, each with a pillared, ginger-breaded porch.

What if Rachel doesn't want to go with him? He has to be

ready with an answer when they call so the choice, when it comes down to it, is job or woman. He could always see her on the weekends, as he's doing now. But realistically, getting from Philadelphia to Queens would be a train and subway marathon, or a drive of stop and go traffic, and the relationship wouldn't survive it. He knows himself.

So he should stay. But the Parkside Food Co-op outgrew its space years ago. And the way it coped was by extending their hours. Traffic in and out of the building was so heavy the five bathrooms had to be cleaned four times a day. While at the Germantown Co-Op there was only one bathroom for members to use and shopping ended at seven every evening and noon time on Sunday. At night the building was cleaned, the equipment scrubbed, the shelves restocked. It didn't happen while the aisles were filled with shoppers.

He decides the job is necessary. He would go even if Rachel didn't join him. Maybe she would join him later, once she sees how things are, once she starts to miss him.

No, he tells himself. New York is the best place for an artist, so why would she want to give it up? They could call any day and offer him the job. He has to be ready.

He reserves a car for the weekend so he can drive down, and as the week drones on, he feels more certain that she will say yes. A man who could give her a life she could devote to her work. A man who already had a good job but was going to be offered a better one. They would have a dog and a vegetable garden. They would have kids. Eventually, she would give up the art and, like his mother, devote herself to family.

Rachel calls in the middle of the week to see if he wants her to get tickets for a movie that weekend. He's evasive. He tells her he's going to be out of town but he doesn't say why. He knows she wants to ask, but she doesn't. He's glad he doesn't have to lie. She'll find out soon. And then she'll be very happy.

13

She's tried to paint but she can't. The emptiness of the canvas she has framed so exquisitely has too much authority. It speaks so boldly in and of itself she is too timid to interrupt. She tries to trick herself. She covers a frame with masking tape so she won't be afraid to get paint on it. She sponges a canvas with a wash of tea to dull the white intensity, but nothing works. So she gives up. She stacks all the framed canvases, there are twenty, against the far wall. Maybe someday she will be able to work on them. She takes out a pad of newsprint and designs a simple rectangular box. She sets up her saw. As she constructs three boxes from sheets of plywood that have been leaning against her wall for weeks, the studio fills with the scent of sawdust and the noise makes her feel as though, at last, something concrete is happening. They are all the same dimensions, sixteen by twenty-four by twenty-four inches, deep enough that the interior is shadowed.

That's what frees her. The flat canvas is too flat, too in-her-face, but the boxes hold darkness. They can't insist on certainty because already they are shrouded. What does the shroud hide?

A body, of course. His body.

She will give it softness and tenderness, she will heal his broken bones, she will recreate the feelings of that night with curved shapes and deep reds and oranges and yellows, the bright colors of passion, and they will be positioned at the farthest depth of the boxes, lit by a hidden bulb that will make the colors glow.

In the middle ground there will be layers of translucency: sheer strips of fabric, veils, lace, maybe plastic beads or string, and in the foreground there would be a further obstruction, something very fragile, delicate, hardly seen, yet there. She goes to thrift stores and junkyards, collecting fabric and metal and strange discards of unwanted things that catch her eye.

It takes more than a month to finish the three boxes and then she constructs six larger ones. She places the bulbs in different positions, incorporates mirrors, reflecting metal strips, wires of all sorts, and she varies the sense of bodies at the far back by making some of them wave-like, others melting or rotund. With all the reflecting surfaces, the viewer's clarity is obscured. What is real, what is illusion? But nothing matters, only feeling.

The last thing she does is have glass cut into panes the same dimensions as the boxes. She slides them into tiny grooves she's made at the front of each box. Then, she sets them on a shelf on her wall and leaves them plugged in overnight. She returns before dawn and in the dark studio she looks carefully at each one. The top of each box comes off; she hasn't yet closed them permanently, and she makes adjustments here and there to enhance the effect. She closes the lid on each one and then walks from one to the next, peering inside.

Yes, this is it. Hints, clues, reflections, nothing ever fully revealed. A sense that something is hidden, something is missing, something was there once but now is absent. This is what it feels like. She has created the ambiguous space she has occupied ever since his dive off the cliff. It will be a series called *Ever Since*, each box numbered.

14

Angela sends her a text: crab dumplings, scallion dumplings, noodle thread soup? She has to get out. Is eight good?

Rachel cleans, buys a bottle of wine, arranges flowers in a vase, hangs a new box on her living room wall. She hasn't seen her friend in a while and the timing is perfect. By seven-thirty everything is ready. She's been rushing around all day, gathering supplies for her studio, building boxes, paying bills, preparing for her next class, and it feels good to sit down, finally, and do nothing.

She sits across from the new box. It's lit by a spot she has installed on her ceiling, and the interior is rich with color. There are hanging shapes in blues and purples with streaks of yellow and orange peeking through layers of dense paint. From top to bottom, rows of thin silver wire spaced at uneven intervals interrupt the view like bars on a window. She can feel herself tipping into that mysterious space, but the wires hold her back. She can only look, she can't enter. It's the predicament he has put her into, the predicament she's accepted. She closes her eyes and drifts into sleep. Minutes later, the buzzer sounds.

While her friend climbs the stairs to the fourth floor, she lights a fire under the steamer. Angela shrugs out of her coat, steps out of her shoes, and sets her bags on the counter. Rachel unpacks the dumplings and arranges the soft pouches in the bamboo baskets. Then she empties the soup into a saucepan. She joins Angela on the couch. They stare at the new box and Angela says, "Wow, I like it. It's so strange. The beauty of it pulls you in, but it keeps you out at the same time. I love the depth, the contrast of colors, and oh!" Angela stands up and approaches the box to peer more closely. "God! That blue is so dense, so layered with all those other colors peeking through!

And then that startling silver wire, so thin, so violent almost. It cuts through, slicing and dividing and keeping you from seeing the whole space. It's like my relationship with Dietrich, you know what I mean?"

Rachel smiles. It is so good to see her friend, to hear her mind at work. It's fast and precise, like her fingers. "No," she says flatly. "I thought it was going well. Last time we talked you said Dietrich was making noises about wanting to see you every weekend. Which sounded sort of like a commitment."

"Well, it wasn't," Angela says. "That beautiful man, and I do mean it, those big eyes, the body. He's like a building. Solid. Rounded corners. Perfectly coordinated parts. And then it's draped in his beautiful clothes. Classy, expensive stuff. We study each other, we're so different. He's like a specimen. But that was only at first. When I got to know him, when I got to love him, that disappeared, and he became a person. Not a German person. Not a ruddy, red-cheeked male who liked to drink absurdly expensive wine, but Dietrich, a very particular person. But for him, I'm still the specimen. Chinese. Living with grandmother. Raised in a foreign neighborhood that he's interested in exploring, using me as the guide."

"How do you know? How can you tell what he's really thinking?"

"Well, that's an absurd question if I ever heard one. Don't let them get too overdone. They'll fall apart."

They move to the table. Rachel lights the candles, tops off their glasses.

Angela sits down across from her and lifting her glass to take a sip says, "I can read it in his face. That's how. Also, he wants ownership. That's the other thing I can read and that's tied into the specimen. He wants to own this Chinese woman, have her all to himself because she's like a fine piece of clothing, another, in his mind, beautiful thing to have in his possession.

"So if I can't make it, he gets annoyed. Not a lot, but peevish, fidgety. What would I have going on that's more important than him? Well, I have my artist life. Shows to go to, studio visits to make. And since I work full time, weekends and nights are when I do my own work. So fuck him."

"I'll drink to that," Rachel says, lifting her glass. "Fuck him!"

"Dusty?" Angela asks.

"Dusty. Something's going on. He's been really evasive. He's away this weekend, but he wouldn't say where or why. I think there's someone else. And that's okay. I could tell he wasn't fully involved." She hears herself say this and realizes she could be talking about herself too. But it's Angela who puts it into words.

"Are *you*?"

"Oh, Angela, you're such a good friend. I really love you."

"So, what's the answer?"

"Sometimes I think I am. But then, he does something that's really cheesy romantic, you know? And I sort of have to work at feeling it. You know what I mean?"

"Like what does he do?"

"Okay. There's this song by the Everly Brothers that he plays. Do you know it? It's so beautiful. 'Let It Be Me'. Here, I'll play it for you." Rachel finds the song on her laptop and they listen.

"That's nice. But I see how it could be too much if you're not into it. Like cake that's too sweet."

"Exactly. He was so moony-faced. But I wasn't ready. I mean, I haven't even seen where this guy lives."

"But you know about it, right? It's a community house for Buddhists. Hasn't he told you about that?"

"He has, I know all about it. But it's not a prison, he could invite me over. I could see the place and it would be like a way of inviting me into his life. But he shuts me out. He keeps me outside."

"But have you ever thought that maybe you're doing the same with him? Maybe he's just following your lead."

"He's been here a hundred times, Angela. He's even been to my studio."

"There's lots of ways of keeping people away."

"I don't know. I certainly found the song annoying because it was too soon. We weren't there yet."

"Excuse me for saying this, but I think you're out of your mind. Dusty is such a good person. He's so generous and thoughtful and he's really spiritual. Dedicated, observant."

"He's not observant. Just about every time he comes over I have a new piece hanging on the wall and he never looks at it."

"Well, he doesn't know squat about art. He's a country kid."

"That's okay. I don't only make my work for other artists. I make it for ordinary people like him. But he doesn't see it. Or if he sees it, because how could he not, right, it doesn't penetrate his brain that it's mine and he should look at it if he cares about me. And I think he does. But he's obtuse. Like I said, he doesn't see."

"Can I say something?"

"You're going to anyway. So, of course, go ahead."

"I think I know what's holding you back."

"Then tell me. Because he's everything you mentioned and sex is good and that's huge, as you know."

Angela doesn't answer. Instead, she looks at Rachel and waits. And Rachel, who knows exactly what Angela is going to say, gives a nod.

"Rubiat. You have to finish with Rubiat."

15

But Angela doesn't know the whole story. She thinks he simply dropped out of school.

Her studio, that February day, is empty. The boxes have gone to a gallery for a show. Seven would be displayed on the walls and there would be three in storage in case clients wanted to see others. She misses them. They made her dreams and desires visible. Now she has to start all over again, and maybe she's ready for the flat world of the canvas.

Rubiat Elsayem, the hard syllables of the first name combined with the flowing syllables of the second. She pictures simple flat surfaces. No mystery. There is enough mystery without her adding to it. Could he be alive? She goes to the Forty-Second Street library and finds the Dansville, New York, newspaper on microfilm. The *Dansville Gazette*. She remembers how she had deceived the reporter who called her. She scrolls back six years and then reads forward, looking for news about the park. But it is only stolen picnic tables, graffiti in the restrooms, crowds on Memorial Day, a child injured at the swimming pool. There is no mention of unidentified bodies, so maybe he's alive.

She makes sketches of the letter R. It is a K with a lid, or a T with a leg and a bosom. She draws ivy garlanding the R and the letter itself disappears. It is like the castle in the fairy tale, covered with ivy and hidden behind briars. The curved shape at the top she turns into a window that peeks out from the ivy-draped structure. She imagines a mind inhabiting the window, but when she thinks about the head it might exist within, she draws a blank. She is too hurt, too angry. Better to stick to symbols. By the end of the week there are two paintings of Rs hanging on the wall, one R is hidden, shadowed, and far away, the other is blazing with color, standing in the foreground.

She begins sketching the letters E and L. E is an all-purpose letter. It's everyday, everywhere, lacking in mystery. Crucial, yet soft in sound. It's curious that his last name, like his first, has three distinct syllables. It takes time to say those words. Rachel Goodwin goes by quickly, but Rubiat Elsayem is labored. You have to say it with intention. Dusty, on the other hand, is a whisper.

Weeks later, one wall in her studio is covered with Rs in various degrees of presence and obscurity, and another wall has a few Els. Maybe they're studies for paintings, she doesn't know, but for now she's working on paper. She's been noticing billboards. Walking or riding the subway, she pays attention to the way certain words are elevated to importance. Messmer Chevrolet standing above the tracks, pasted against the sky. Not even night obscures them because billboards have lights. Elsayem Chevrolet. Elsayem Liquors. What was the mother's business? But she didn't have Rubiat's name. *Ms. Elsayem*, she had said, *I'm sorry for your loss*, and the woman had replied, *I never married Rubiat's father*. So, what was *her* name? She doesn't remember. Yet that name also started with El, she is sure of it.

The store was on the Upper West Side. She remembers thinking it was a tony address. But it wasn't on an avenue, it was a cross street. And what was the most well-known cross street? Seventy-Second was a major subway stop and it had the Museum of Natural History on its corner. Of course! It was a shop that started with the El sound on Seventy-Second Street.

That evening she takes the train into Manhattan and gets off at Seventy-Second. She walks up to Central Park West on the north side and down on the south side. Then she crosses Broadway and walks down to West End, but there are fewer shops. Still, to be thorough, she walks all the way up, but nothing there begins with El.

Maybe it isn't Seventy-Second Street after all. She takes the subway up to Ninety-Sixth and stands on the corner of Broadway, looking up the sidewalk toward Amsterdam. Traffic goes both ways and that would be better for businesses getting deliveries, surely, and each side of the street is lined with shops. She walks up the incline on the south side, and there it is. Elsinora Shoes. It has two storefronts with large glass windows displaying shoes and boots for men and women. The prices aren't posted which makes her suspect they are expensive. The sign, hanging from a metal arm perpendicular to the windows is a rectangular box with an orange background that sizzles in the dark behind scripted black letters that also march across the top of the windows, *Italian Imports* below. She peers past the display into the dark interior. Maybe Rubiat himself works there. She is glad she's come after it's closed. To see him, even to see someone who is related to him, she will need to prepare. She can't be needy and emotional.

That night Dusty comes to her apartment. He arrives with a bouquet. "How pretty. What's the occasion?"

"It's a long story. Let's talk over dinner. I'm hungry."

"Where do you want to go?"

"Somewhere quiet and cozy."

That ruled out Jiang Nan, a popular Chinese restaurant where the wait was long and the dining rooms, several on each of the three floors, were noisy. "I've never been, but there's a small Middle Eastern restaurant a couple blocks away. You can't fuck up hummus, right? I just want soup anyway."

"Trust me, you can," Dusty says. But they go. There are only a few tables and the number of helmeted cyclists going in and out, carrying black insulated bags shaped to strap onto their cycles, explains it. They choose a table as far away from the door as they can get and a girl who looks about sixteen brings them tea and sets their places.

Dusty says, "Let's just get a combination platter, we can share it, and how about two soups? I'll get the lentil, you?"

"Sounds good." He is looking at her so strangely she blurts out, "What's going on with you? Where have you been?"

He grins. He's trimmed his beard, he's even shaved his neck, and he looks like a proper and disciplined member of society, rather than a lumber man, his normal persona. He reaches into his pocket and sets a tiny velvet box on the table. His fingernails are scrubbed and clean. He keeps them long for playing the guitar, and they often have a line of dirt, as though he is still a farmer working in soil. "Open it," he says.

She opens the lid, but she knows what it will be before she sees it. She can't control her face. First the song, now this.

"You're not happy?"

"I'm startled. I wasn't expecting it. In fact, if you really want to know, I was getting a little suspicious. You've been so, I don't know, so secretive. These mysterious trips? What's going on?"

"I can explain. But I wanted you to know, upfront, what I'm thinking. You don't have to give an answer, I know this is sudden. And you need to know everything before you commit because I don't want you to feel trapped later. But this is how I've been thinking about...well...us."

"Stop talking riddles." She can't help her abrupt tone. Another man with a mystery.

Their soups arrive, big steaming bowls of red broth, deliciously spiced, with chopped mint floating on top.

"I've accepted a job in Philadelphia to manage a small co-op in a really interesting part of the city, very old, with big, old houses you can rent for cheap, called Germantown." Her face tells him nothing. "It's a food co-op," he explains.

"But why would you go from the biggest co-op in the country to a small one? And trade Philadelphia for New York? I mean, isn't it sort of a demotion?"

"Not at all. They really like me. They really want me. It's better pay, full benefits, and I'll be the manager. Rachel, it's not a behemoth. It's reasonable, slow-paced. It's going to suit me. You can fit your mind around it, less stress, and it's a better quality life there overall. I think you'd like it. We could find a place to rent that would include a whole floor for your studio. Big stone houses, they're very old, like seventeen, eighteen hundreds. Porches, big backyards. You could have a garden, a dog, maybe even chickens, I don't know. I'd like you to come with me. That's what the ring signifies." There, he's said it.

"I'm sorry, I don't know what to say. I'm sort of stunned. When does it start?"

"Three months. But you wouldn't have to come right away. You could take your time, check it out, spend a week there or something. It's such a cool neighborhood, you won't believe it."

"I have a rent stable apartment, Dusty."

"You could sublet it for a month and come with me. I really think you'd like it."

"Are you trying to convince me?"

"Of course, what's wrong with that?"

"Don't be a salesman. This is my life."

"It's my life too," he says softly, his voice scratchy, tears ready to spill.

"I can't give you a yes or no answer."

"Of course, I realize that."

"I can't take the ring right now because I don't know, Dusty, it's all just—" She looks down at the table, trying to protect him. "—very sudden."

"Maybe you could try it, see if it fits." He says this in a pleading, needy voice. His nose is leaking, water tipping from his eyes, he feels like he's seven years old.

When she lifts it off the satin cushion, she's startled at how little it weighs, and peering closely, sees that the diamond is ringed with rubies. It's a small, humble diamond, not showy or imposing. She slips the band on her finger and it fits perfectly. But she slips it off and sets it back in the box. When he puts it back in his pocket, she feels his agony. Why has she treated this decent, kind, good man so awfully?

"I've learned the words and I've been practicing."

He knows what she's referring to. But he can't move on.

"Dusty, listen to me. I love you, I do."

"I'm sorry." It's pathetic to say this. But he feels ashamed. He's made a terrible mistake, he's read her all wrong.

16

At noon the next day she walks into Elsinora Shoes. The interior has soft, muted colors; spots on the ceiling illuminate the glossy leathers arranged in racks around the two rooms. One side is men's footwear, the other women's. An elegant gray-haired man looks up from the desk in the back and tells her to take her time and look around. He would be happy to help her when she is ready. She finds the price on the soles of the shoes and quickly realizes there isn't anything under three hundred dollars. In her ratty puffer coat, a grubby, much-used backpack over her shoulders, he will know, right away, she can't afford expensive footwear, so she won't even pretend. Instead, she walks up to him and holds out her hand. "Sorry, I'm not here to shop. My name is Rachel Goodwin."

He is gracious even before she explains her purpose, giving her his soft, manicured hand, and tilting his head in deference saying, "Very pleased to meet you. Matteo Elsinora." His lack of suspicion seems almost un-American.

"I went to school with Rubiat and I met Ms. Elsinora when she came to Crandall, and we talked a bit. I was a good friend and I've always wondered what happened to Rubiat."

"Ah." Matteo sighs. "Trust me, it's quite a complicated story. He hasn't been in touch with you?"

"Well, that's the problem. I have a different email and cell phone and if he wanted to find me, I don't think he could. But I really would like to talk to him. He's alive?"

"Indeed," Matteo says. "I understand."

The bell on the door jingles and a man wheels in a hand truck stacked with boxes.

"Excuse me, please. Why don't you have a seat? This way, sir, right through to the back. Thank you very much." He holds open the door, letting in cold air, and then returns. "So very sorry." She stands, just to be polite, but he says, "Would you like tea, coffee?" And then he sits down next to her and says, "I'm sure Rubiat would be glad to know you've been thinking of him, but the person you really should talk to is my sister. I'm really not the one who knows my nephew's information. It's his mother who's most up to date with things."

She can only repeat her question. "He's alive, then?"

"Oh yes, very much so. Why would you doubt it?"

"I thought maybe there'd been an accident of some kind."

"Not that I know of. But as I say, it's his mother who would be the best person. If you would like to give me your number, I'll pass it on to her and I'm sure she'll be in touch."

"Thank you. I really hope she'll contact me soon."

"Of course," Matteo says kindly. "I do understand. I will be sure to give her your information."

"If it could happen today, that would be great."

But Matteo only nods. Then he stands up and walks her to the door.

Back in her studio, she stretches a new canvas and begins painting. There is a pair of letters, EL, standing high above an abstracted landscape, a suggestion of a city with curved tracks, subway lines perhaps, swirling below it. She uses oranges, yellows, greens, building up a thick surface, but the letters are a gray, pencil-like wash, translucent and insubstantial.

When her phone rings that evening, she is in class. She hears the muted tone in her backpack and knows it's his mother. But she has another half an hour to go, so she puts it out of her mind. The word they are discussing is *wait*. They tell her that in Spanish, esperar, the verb for wait, is also the verb for…they don't know the word in English, but it is to want very much, to pray for it, and she says, you must mean *hope*. "Is it the same in English, to hope and wait—same meaning?"

"No," she says, "they mean different things. I hope she will call me. I wait for the bus. I hope it comes soon. You remember soon? There's soon, late, later, all degrees of time."

She writes the three words on the board and they make up sentences:

"Soon I will speak English."

"Later, I will know what happened."

"She is late to call me."

They are confused about the word *will*, so she assigns the chapter on the future tense and draws a diagram on the board. It is a stick figure standing in a slot called now, present time. It walks toward the future, which is called, what *will* happen.

"Can the figure walk backward into the past?" She points to the grandmother. She had signed up for her class again and asks the question more slowly. "Can this person go back to, return to her past?"

The grandmother shakes her head and says no. Then she adds, "She can in, how you call? Sleep stories?"

"Sleep stories? Oh, of course! We call sleep stories *dreams*. And yes, you can, sort of, in dreams. Are there any other ways?"

"By remember," the grandmother says, and her grandson chirps, "Memory!"

"Good answer!" Rachel writes memory in the slot called the past. "Memory is the only true way she can return to the past."

Instead of gathering her things when the class is over and leaving with her students, all of them clomping down the stairs through the empty building, she stays in the room and looks at her phone. Unknown caller. She calls the number and as soon as she hears the voice, she remembers that long-ago meeting and how uncomfortable the woman had made her feel.

"Hello, Rachel. My brother told me you'd like to contact Rubiat. What I suggest is that we meet at a coffee shop. By that time, I would know how Rubiat wants to proceed."

"Couldn't you just give me his number, or even just his email, and let me contact him?"

"'I'm afraid I can't do that. This is the best way, trust me.'"
Matteo had also asked her to trust him. Such a peculiar expression. Who says it but people who have something to hide? The next day she receives an email proposing a date, place, and time and she accepts. They will meet for lunch at the restaurant on the sixth floor of Macy's. Rachel has the uneasy sensation and later, dread, of an interview. She could rebel and go in the old clothes she wears to her studio, or she could put effort into it and dress to please. It's tempting to do the former, but she knows it would only antagonize an already difficult woman, so she gets an outfit ready. She even finds a string of fake pearls.

17

They haven't spoken in two months, and when she sees that it's her brother, she clicks on the call, full of the pleasure of hearing his voice. It's careful and measured, as always, but she detects a hint of something else, something excited.

"I asked her out."

"Wait a minute, who?"

"Ruby, that woman I was telling you about, remember?"

"Right, right, of course! And?" But now she can feel him backing up. Her brother is always strategic. That's why he'd chosen Ann. She was a proper kind of woman who came from the same proper upper middle-class background he did, and sameness was important to him. Ann would blend in.

"We went out to dinner."

"What was she wearing?"

"You're so predictable," he says. "She was wearing this unbelievably sexy black sweater kind of thing."

"Which you took off her later, right?"

"Just wait. And we had a nice dinner at a really nice restaurant. Talked for a long time, drank wine. We sat close," he clears his throat, "legs touching. She invited me back to her place. She has a roommate but apparently she was gone and…"

"And?" Rachel asks.

"I have to see her again. It was fabulous."

"You fucked?"

"We fucked," Edward says, laughing.

Her big brother, always so afraid to step outside of order was finally making a mess. "Congratulations. So, are you rethinking things with Ann?"

"Too many questions," Edward replies. "I'll call you later."

18

Clouds hang over the city. Sidewalks stretch into a foggy distance where they meld into a gray horizon, but inside Macy's it is bright with color and loud, reckless extravagance. As she takes one escalator after another up to the sixth floor, she sees aerial views of a glitzy commerce that feels alien to everything in her life. It is predominantly women's clothing, racks and racks of it, hundreds, maybe thousands of things to wear. She can't imagine who buys it all.

The sixth floor is bedding, big puffy quilts on model beds that stand under harsh lights, wholesome, colorful patterns suggesting happy lives. The restaurant is in a far corner and she feels nervous as she walks toward it. There would never be a lunch rush up here. This restaurant is for special occasions or people who want to impress. It's a peculiar choice, she thinks, but maybe his mother comes here often. Maybe it's the haunt of rich, lonely women.

She gives her name to the hostess and is led past empty tables with sparkling glasses and silverware to a distant window where a severe middle-aged woman sits in celestial light. She recognizes her once they get closer, but the woman's expression doesn't change, and needing to look somewhere else, she notices that the linen napkins are folded into parasols at each place setting, an amusing extravagance she likes.

The lips turn up slightly, her concession to a smile, and the greeting, stated crisply, sails forth. "Rachel, it's good to see you."

"Ms. Elsinora, thank you for inviting me." She sits down, lays the napkin in her lap, takes a sip of ice water, and looks at her companion, noticing the careful makeup, the stylishly colored hair, the sparkle of her nails. Icy and perfect. She wants to ask right away if she's talked to him, but the old lady is in charge and she has to wait, esperar. And hope, esperar.

"Did you graduate from that art school?"

"Yes, I did. It feels like a long time ago."

"And do you work as an artist now? Do you sell your art?"

"I do work as an artist and I'm having my first one-person show at a gallery right now. But even if I sell some pieces, it's not enough to live on, so I also teach English as a second language. I'm based in Queens. That's where my apartment and studio are."

"I see. What is the name of the gallery, if I may ask?"

"Sure. It's not a Fifty-Seventh Street gallery, but it is in Manhattan. White Pillars. It's a very well-respected gallery so I feel lucky to have a show there. It's the kind of place where people like me can get their start."

"Very good. I know Rubiat will be very happy to hear all of this and I certainly will tell him."

"Actually, I'd like to tell him myself. Did he say I could contact him?"

"Oh, dear. I'm sorry if I gave you the wrong impression. Did you think I was going to ask?"

"Well, I was hoping you'd ask." She thinks of Dusty and the engagement ring. Then she thinks of her boxes, intricate visuals for the eye to travel into, to find the answer it needs. But this woman stands in the way and after all her work, it angers her. What gives her that right? "I don't understand why I can't approach him myself. He's an adult. I mean, has something happened that I don't know about?"

"Rubiat is doing very well, thank you. But the reason I wanted to meet you first is simple. I remember very well who you are. I remember that snake and, frankly, I believe you should stay away from my son. I don't think you'd be good for him. I don't think you'd have his best interests at heart. You see, I can tell what sort of person you are, and I know, from personal experience, that in romance, the person in love, or hoping to be in love, is often not the best judge. And I suspect you don't know much about love yourself. I suspect you use men as opportunity, and having been in a relationship like that, I know the signs. I don't want Rubiat to suffer the way I've suffered."

The waiter comes for their order, but Rachel hasn't looked at the menu, and isn't sure she'll be able to eat, so she orders the soup of the day. A quick glance around the room surprises her. All those empty tables are now occupied and more people are waiting at the front of the restaurant.

"They have a very nice quiche here; that's what I often have. Are you sure soup is all you want?"

"Yes, thank you." As soon as the server leaves Rachel says, "Does Rubiat know you're interfering?"

"I am simply doing what parents used to do all the time."

"For their daughters maybe. Back in the Dark Ages. But this is America, the twenty-first century and he's a son."

"I don't think it matters. He is my child and we have always been good friends."

"All I want is to talk to him. I don't even know what he's been doing or where he's living. And I want him to know where I am. Talking is nothing to worry about."

"I realize that. I understand."

"I think he liked me."

"But he was leaving. So he didn't like you enough to stay. He must have had an intuition because he's doing very well now and, frankly, he doesn't need a person in his life who thinks he's a snake."

"That was an assignment, it has nothing to do with my feelings for him. I used the snake for other qualities. Long and thin and the ability to hide."

"I see. Well, there is also your brashness, your lack of humility or elegance."

"Do you know that Everly Brothers song, 'Let It Be Me?' Do you listen to music? Is music important to you?"

"Oh yes, in my family we listen to Italian opera. Rubiat was raised on opera, you see."

And she *can* see. Right away, she understands how such exaggerated drama and passion has formed him. And in that context, maybe the dive makes more sense. And then she says, "You should choose me for your son." It is the word *choose* that initiates it, and then impulse takes over, and just like him, she chooses not to edit it. She stands up. She can see, now, that there is a bar on the opposite wall, with shelves of bottles reflected in a mirror, and diners sitting at a curved counter. People are busy looking at menus, chatting with one another, unfolding napkins on their laps. She will give them an experience. Imagining Dusty sitting beside her, playing the guitar, she opens her mouth and then, with a startled heart beating beneath her dress, she sings their song in full-throated abandon, sending her voice over the music, over their heads, filling the busy room with the certainty of her feelings. So many faces looking up, so many happy, startled expressions.

I bless the day I found you
I want to stay around you
And so I beg you, let it be me

At the second verse, Ms. Elsinora gets to her feet and hisses, "All right, that's enough. Sit, sit, this is ridiculous. Sit down now!"

But Rachel keeps on going. She sings all six verses and when she gets to the end...

So never leave me lonely
Tell me you love me only
And that you'll always—let—it—be—me

Waiters and customers applaud. She nods, as a thanks, and notices that someone turned off the music.

But the bitch is stony faced. Rachel tells her, sitting down, "The lover sings that to his or her beloved, but I sang it to my beloved's mother. Imagine that! If I were your son, I'd be furious that you were meddling." She sees the waiter approach with their food and before he reaches their table she says, "I have to go now," and as she walks through the tables, people nod to her, someone says, "Well done!" A young woman touches her arm. "That was fantastic, I'll never forget it. Neither will he."

"I won't," her companion says, "thank you."

19

Their routine is to have coffee and cornetti delivered to the shop and go over the accounts every morning as they sit at a table in the stock room. They are scrupulous about crumbs, protecting their laps and chests with large cloth napkins they keep at the shop for that purpose. Bibbed like infants, that is why they sit in the back room out of sight.

They are good friends, these siblings, and since both live alone and both have been orphaned by a large extended family where there were aunts, uncles, and parents, but no cousins, it is just the two of them now that the old people have died. They suffer with the peculiar burden of children who have been spoiled by so many doting adults. That burden of love manifested in both of them as entitlement. They want what they want when they want it, and their aggression has paid off in the shoe trade. Theirs is the only shop on the west side that has direct accounts in Milan, Rome, and Florence with the bootmakers themselves and not distributors. They get what they want and they get it quickly because Matteo speaks a proper, formal Italian, not the Americanized Italian of most first generations who have picked it up during childhood. Matteo learned to speak from a tutor he'd hired as an adult, a man from a good family in Milan who also kept an apartment in Manhattan.

This winter, men's boots are selling well, but women's boots are slowing down. Their solution is to raise the price on all women's styles 10 percent. Discount is an American word that has never crossed their lips. In addition, the words "sale" and "reduced" have never been uttered within the four walls of Elsinora Shoes. They dislike crowds and prefer it when there are no more than four people in the shop. It is this more European attitude that is the reason for their success. They cater to the upper class. Their footwear never goes out of style and what doesn't sell one year will sell the next. Classic, enduring, perennial: these are the words that define their business.

"Matti, the girl called."

"What did she want?"

"She wanted Rubi's number, but I put her off. I met her for lunch. I needed to speak to her, you know, get a sense of what she wanted. A phone number is an open door and maybe you don't want an open door."

"Absolutely." He pours himself a second cup of espresso, and takes a warm cornetto from the basket, wiping his fingers after touching the buttery surface. "Did she say why she wanted to contact him?"

"Well, she's a young woman with very definite ideas."

"Like them all."

"But she seems to have some kind of plan involving Rubi. She told me I was interfering in his life and if he knew he would be furious. She stood up in the restaurant, right at our table, as though she were some kind of singer."

"What? To sing something?"

"Yes, it was a song that was very romantic. People clapped."

"Really? That's extraordinary! Did you appreciate it?"

"No, I did not. I was embarrassed. How can I go back there?"

"But that sounds marvelous. It sounds operatic."

"No, no, it wasn't a classical song. It was some kind of pop song, a country song probably, I certainly didn't recognize it."

"Fantastic! I wish I had been there."

"It's true, you should have been there. You would have done much better than me." She helps herself to a cornetto, and breaking it in half, the soft, buttery dough spiraling out, says, "Matti, tell me the truth, was I interfering?"

"You tell me."

"I was. I was. I feel so ashamed. But I was only...you know how it is."

"He's twenty-six years old, Leni. He's not your little boy anymore. You can't protect him from harm."

"I should just give her his number. Right away. I should text it to her. I know I should, but I hesitate. It would feel like handing her a signed, blank check. Or at the very least, a recommendation. When the last thing I want is for him to think I approve of this particular female. And he would see it that way, I know he would."

Matteo has the same instinct to protect as his sister, so he says, "Let me call Rubi. Let's see what he wants us to do."

"Thank you." Leni eats her cornetto, leaning over the plate so all the buttery flakes fall where they should. Then she wipes her mouth, her fingers, and gets up to wash their dirty dishes. Her brother is a better partner in life than a husband ever could be. She walks through the darkened shop, turning on lights, and Matteo unlocks the front door.

PART TWO

IMPULSE

20

The view from the top takes his breath away. The hills stretch into the distance, their purple tops and wooded sides softened by mist, their farther reaches hidden by clouds. Below him, it is a dizzy swirl of green broken by the sharp grays of rock in the streambed. How absurd to stand on this ledge, barefoot, and lift up as though he were standing on a diving board over a pool of shimmery blue water. He raises his hands over his head and lifts up on his toes, and then, because the end is already determined, he enters the quiescent, supple medium of sky. He has craved this surge of freedom, and now that he's in the air, he is relieved there is no going back, no revising the impulse. It makes him giddy with happiness, his great long lumbering body sailing through the air. He comes down on a sapling that grows out from the wall at a horizontal tilt. His arms and shoulders take the landing. There is a shooting pain as his body crashes through branches that break underneath him and drop him onto the wall of cliff where there is nothing but shale. He slides, face down, fast, and comes to a stop at another tree growing horizontally with a nest of branches pointing upward toward the sun, pinning him in their tangle. He blacks out, and when he wakes up, he is in a war movie. A helicopter swings in the air, shattering the stillness. He can see a man with binoculars and he tries to wave, but his brain isn't connected to his arms and his will seems to have departed. He is hollow, there is no self, and the roaring machine fills the husk of his body.

Consciousness comes back when the moon is at the top of the sky, a great white lamp bleaching the darkness. Something trickles into his brain, but he can't identify it. Knowledge? Determination? He tries to chase it away. He prefers the state of not being, not wanting, not feeling. But he is aware of sensation slowly spreading through his numbed and battered body. It is the accretion of purpose, and soon he finds his legs, his feet, his arms and then he is sitting upright. Then he is climbing out of the nest, sliding down the sheer rock face, out of control, nothing to grab onto. He digs in with his feet, but it is as fast as ice and he must give in or get destroyed. He slams into the rock on the walkway sideways. His feet are bleeding, his arms are scratched, his shoulders ache. He curls into a ball, knees to his chest, and tries to disappear. But will is supreme, and when daybreak comes, he wakes to purple light and stumbles down the path till he comes to the swimming pool she had talked about, a vast concrete pit.

He collapses on the stone bench facing it. The sky loses the exhilaration of dawn as the grayness of morning slides across. He hurts all over, but once again, the duty to continue, to be alive insists itself when what he wants is oblivion. He closes his eyes, attempting to call it back. But time shoulders in and soon, he can hear the sound of cars on a distant road. He lifts his eyes to the concrete pit where a puddle of water has collected leaves. He sees the steel gates at either end that are closed in the summer and he imagines Rachel swimming here with her family. And then he brings his glance to the stone apron where he sits and there are sneakers, socks, and a scarf. His. How is that possible? He stares at them, uncomprehending. He closes his eyes, but daylight insists, and he must open them again. He stands up. The shoes call to him, an unknown authority, and he obeys. He pulls socks over his torn and bloodied feet and then slips each one into the familiar house of a shoe that once, a long time ago, was his. He cleans his hands and face with wet leaves, runs his fingers through his hair, shaking out the grit and stone, then he re-ties it with the rubber. He brushes dirt off his clothes, trying to make himself presentable. His body feels bruised, his feet are painful, his shoulders ache.

Now he stands on the side of the road with his thumb out, trying to catch a ride north, into the unknown. A rusted pickup stops for him and as he runs toward it, limping, he feels the thrill of impulse. Not even a fall toward death can wipe it out, it rises inside him with the same reckless glee and irreverence of an erection that appears at an inconvenient moment. The driver is Rubiat's age, a kid with long dirty blond hair, who says, "Where you going man?" and Rubiat answers, "Where can you take me?"

The kid laughs. "Rochester Community College, on 15A. That a help to you?"

"Perfect," Rubiat says, "exactly where I wanted to go myself."

"No kidding, you go there too?"

"Not yet, but I want to. What are you studying?"

"Engine repair. Cars, tractors, lawnmowers, anything, but mostly cars and trucks."

"Good school?"

"Not bad, not too expensive. Classes never too big."

Abel finds a parking slot, then slings his bag over his shoulder and bolts toward the buildings. He's late for class but he's given Rubiat his number and suggested they have a beer later.

Rubiat stands in a vast ocean of macadam, looking in the direction Abel and other students walk toward, where a cluster of low buildings squat under the morning sky. He has survived once again; he feels lucky. As he walks toward the buildings, following everyone else, his limp improves, but the tender spots on his feet where they were abraded by rock, are painful.

In the bathroom he washes his face properly, dries it with paper towels, wishes he had a razor. He exits, finds a bench outside, sits down and looks across gleaming metallic acres of cars. The campus oppresses him. It is too rational. Low-maintenance plantings frame all-purpose buildings that could contain offices, shops, or apartments. Nothing distinguishes them as classrooms. Nevertheless, it's the place he's come to, and because he's a person who lacks volition or even purpose, it's what he has.

By the end of the day, he has walked down countless lino-
leum-tiled hallways, filled out forms in triplicate, posed for a
camera and purchased books and classes in plumbing, an area
of study in the Skilled Trades Department that will earn him a
certificate. A week later, he is living in an apartment near the
college and owns a student-inspected, twenty-year-old sedan
with a student-rebuilt engine he has purchased from the auto-
motive department with the help of Abel.

He studies, pays his rent, and does what his teachers tell him
to. But he stays aloof. The only person he knows as a friend is
Abel, but Abel's idea of fun is to go to a bar and get wasted.
After the first two times, Rubiat stops answering his calls.

He makes a life. He is glad to have escaped the pretensions
of art school by expressing himself in the only authentic way
possible: spontaneous risk-taking, and rather than feeling like
a victim of his impulses, he begins to understand them as op-
portunities. Each has taken him into the unknown. Each has
provided a map he can't see but knows is the course correction
he must follow.

One evening, standing in his empty apartment, he realizes
it was Rachel who put his shoes on the walkway. He knows
full well that if he hadn't been wearing shoes, no one would
have picked him up, not even Abel. The shoes made everything possible. He feels her presence, her warm, sturdy body,
her strong back and shoulders, her hair absolutely straight and
thick. He hears her scream. He feels her horror and then he is
overcome with shame as he sees what she must have seen, a
silly guy in green pants pretending he was on a diving board.
And yet, this person who had every right to be angry at him,
left the shoes that had opened all the subsequent doors. It is
because of her selflessness, her care, her understanding, that he
owns five different wrenches and knows how to use them, that
he can install toilets and sinks and fix leaks, that he can go into
a basement and look at a complex network of pipes and understand how the water is carried to each appliance in the house. A
plumber works with invisible things. He sees stuff no one else

bothers with and what most people take for granted are the very things he attends to. He makes sure water will always gush out when a faucet is opened, that fittings are secure, lines clear, and nothing can freeze. And if he doesn't know these things now, he will know them soon, before he gets his certificate. A plumber is a person who creeps about in places where spiders cling and mildew grows, basements, crawl spaces, all the wet, mouse-dropped undersides of contemporary life. He's learning the secrets. Best of all, everything he does is based on logic and observation. Logic determines cause and effect and makes the unknown knowable.

The college is in Brighton, a suburb on the south side of Rochester. The buildings occupy a three-hundred-acre clearing that is, itself, a smaller clearing within a tremendous acreage that once was covered with trees and pasture. Now, everything has been rolled smooth for the molasses-like topping of macadam. When winter comes, gleeful winds spin the snow horizontally, obscuring the flat commercial sprawl of roads and malls. They call it a white-out and nothing shuts the city down faster. Classes are cancelled and Rubiat must stay in his second-floor apartment in Lilac Gardens, a building of hollow walls and plywood floors covered with thin commercial carpet, and on his own, study flow, compression, vacuum.

Lilac Gardens is directly across from the school. He owns a chair, a table, a mattress, a few pots and dishes, nothing that isn't essential. Which also defines the whole of his life. As wind spins the snow into cyclones that blanket his windows, he thinks about the impulses, how each had been at a threshold moment. The first was getting his driver's license, that had made a whole new world accessible. Sex with Rachel was the second. It was the first time he had felt love for a woman. The third threshold, getting his plumber's certificate, is less than six months away. If he wants to survive it, he will have to be strategic and take great care. At the very least, he should avoid highways and cliffs.

21

Across from the college there is a low, tan brick building with a sign out front: Monroe Counseling Center. He parks in the lot and walks through the front door into a reception area where a woman sits at a desk answering phone calls. When she looks up at him he says, "How many therapists work here?"

"At the moment, because two are on vacation, there are four: Joseph, Petrovia, Lattimore, and Allarkeny. You can read their bios here." She hands him a glossy sheet with photos and text.

He folds it and slips it into his pocket. "Who has the next available appointment?"

"For today?"

"Yes, soon if that's possible."

"Normally, they're all booked up, but someone had a cancellation, I think. Let's see. Yes, that would be Ms. Lattimore. Room five in twenty minutes. Would you like to take that slot?"

Her name is Donna. He's relieved to discover that she's past middle age and elegant in a matronly way, not someone he would be attracted to. She looks at his face as they talk and doesn't take a lot of notes. Nor is there a computer or recording device in sight.

The first session is merely a chance to meet and collect essential facts and when he pays the receptionist, he feels cheated. She notices that. "I know," she says, "and I agree totally. The first session should be done over the phone so there's no charge."

But the next session feels more substantial. Donna begins by asking, "Can you describe for me what brings you to counseling?"

He tells her about the impulse events.

"Interesting," she says, and he struggles to contain his disappointment. Interesting? Because something like this isn't in the textbooks?

But then she asks, "Have there been other impulses, less dramatic, less dangerous, ones that might have slipped by your attention?" He has to think about that. He realizes the answer is yes, everything he is doing now is the result of impulse. Going to Rochester, enrolling in school, buying the particular car he has. Even choosing her as his therapist. He simply took what offered itself. "I'm not the kind of person who researches things or asks people's opinion. Something comes along, I grab it."

"Interesting. So, is there nothing you haven't done spontaneously?"

"I have to think about that," he says, looking down at the carpet, a brown and tan weave that is identical to the carpeting in his apartment.

"While you're thinking," she says, "tell me about your parents. Let's take your father first."

"Nada," he replies.

"He wasn't around?"

"All I know about him is his name. I have his name, Elsayem. He was Ahmed."

"And your mother?"

"A very private woman. Proud, punctual, organized. She provided a stable existence and I love her very much. What happened between her and my father I don't know. Does he even know I exist?" He shrugs.

"Have you ever tried to locate him?"

"What would be the point? I'm loyal to my mother. It was her choice not to tell me about him and I want to respect that."

"But how do you picture him?"

"I don't," he says.

She is flustered for just a moment. Then she says, "Surely you see someone when you think of Ahmed Elsayem."

"I see a place. I see Moorish architecture, a mosque, a desert.

Some kind of North African place. Like Morocco. And I see this clichéd Arab man, flowing robes, horseback. It's a Lawrence of Arabia kind of image. And back to the other question? The decision to go to art school. As I told you, I went for only a semester. But that was something I had researched. I chose the place carefully, considering tuition, location, that sort of thing. And look how it turned out. I was totally wrong about everything. That's what gets me, my lack of, what would you call it, self-knowledge."

"When you get your plumbing certificate, will you take the first job that comes along?"

"I don't think so. I can't live here and most of the jobs seem to be in Rochester."

"What's wrong with Rochester?"

"In my opinion, as a New Yorker, it's not a city. Sorry if that offends."

"I have no fondness for Rochester, don't worry. Where will you go then?"

"I want to be somewhere in the country. Maybe south of here, where the art school is, I'm hoping for that area."

"Why?"

"Emptiness. No malls, few traffic lights. No highways where I might drive too fast and crash my car. I don't know. Just a feeling, really. You either live in a real city or you live in the country. That's my conclusion I guess."

"Okay. That's all our time for now, but this is a good start, and I'll see you next week." When she stands up, she comes to his shoulder. They shake hands.

She begins the next session with a question that surprises him. If he had stayed in art school, what word would he have used to describe her...what was that phrase? She pauses, then supplies it herself: causative factor. And what animal did she make him think of?

He is impressed that she has remembered what he told her,

even down to that odd phrase, and then he is challenged, appropriately, by the question. But then it dawns on him. "Wait a minute...are these sessions being recorded?"

"Absolutely not. I would need your permission for that. I don't record because I don't like to lose the spontaneity of these sessions, which is helpful to both of us."

"Then how'd you remember causative factor?"

"It happens to be in my notes." She looks at him challengingly.

He nods, ashamed for doubting her. Is it because she's a woman, he wonders, and then answers the question. "She was like an owl. I've never seen an owl, but I know they're hunters, nighttime hunters. There's something about their wings that makes them absolutely silent. That's the extent of my owl facts. She was so surprising. No one special, you wouldn't look at her twice, but she was wild. In bed, I mean. Her room was a turret. Windows on every side. A perch. She could see everything. It was like she was tuned into vibrations other people don't know about. Sound, color. But you would guess none of that looking at her. A wide flat face, kind of owl-like now that I think about it. She was friendly. A happy, friendly person. With this hidden wildness. A beautiful body without clothes. With clothes, like I said, you wouldn't look twice. The word I'd choose for her is sympathy. I'd have performed it with big wide gestures. Inclusive gestures. Embraces, smiles, that kind of thing.

"The word I *told* her was comfortable. But at that point, that was the next day, when we were in the park, or going to the park, sometime that next day when I was feeling totally replete, sexually exhausted, that was what she meant to me. Like I was a child, and she was the mother."

"Interesting. That was your feeling when you were standing on the edge of the cliff?"

"Sorry, what do you mean?"

"What were you feeling just before you took the dive?"

"Excited. Powerful. Invincible."

"And before that, you were feeling like you'd been with a mother figure, which is someone who could protect you and care for you, who has your best interests in their heart."

"Yes, I think so. Why?"

"It's a strange way to talk about a woman you've just had wild sex with. A mother? Really?"

"That was the next morning, after waking up. Believe me, I have no desire to have sex with my mother."

"But let's follow this a little more. Allow your associative mind to go where it wants. Great sex, true love, what pops into your head?"

"You really want to know? A feeling like I'm being sucked into an endless space, sort of a black hole, an infinite spiral of blackness. I feel a sense of dread."

"Now, when you were standing on the edge of the cliff, do you remember what you saw in front of you?"

"Wait a minute. Can we slow down? I don't think you're understanding. She had told me that she loved the absurd. And we were talking about surrealism in our class which we defined as things removed from their normal context." He looks at her. Was she following? Did she know anything about art history? She's written a word on her pad. Then she looks up at him, her brown, watery eyes glistening. Even in the dusk of the afternoon light coming through the window her eyes appear watery. He wonders if it's related to sadness in her own life, or if she's merely feeling for him. If the latter, it's a level of empathy he's never seen or even imagined was possible.

"Okay," she says, "go on."

"And I was inspired at that moment. She'd gone away to pee, so I was alone. I pulled off my shoes and socks and you see, we both had been divers in high school, we'd talked about that just before we got to the park. So, I was like a diver, poised on the board, ready to jump. I never intended to jump. Why would I want to dive into a rocky stream bed? I wanted her to come back, not find me, and then see me there, in that absurd moment. I knew she would see it that way. I knew she would.

And I'd left my red scarf next to my shoes so the color would catch her eye. She'd look up from the shoes and she'd see me. And then, suddenly, I was going over. I hadn't intended to do that. I mean, it was an act of suicide. Why would I do that when I'd just found this woman? It doesn't make sense."

"It doesn't make rational sense, not at all. But maybe something else was going on, something from a long time ago, maybe your infancy. Try to replay it in your mind and we'll begin there at our next session."

22

Henry Plumbing and Electric is a small business in a town called Riverville, ten miles from Crandall. Walter Henry, sole proprietor, doesn't have a shop, he has a van filled with tools and parts that rivals a shop. He has been in business for fifty years, fixing the electric and plumbing problems of the residents of three counties, traveling so many miles each year he has to replace a set of tires every fifteen months. Now, at age seventy-nine, he is looking for a partner to take over the plumbing side of the business. He's too old to crawl around under houses, too tired of messing with feces that gurgle up into toilet bowls and overflow onto bathroom floors. He's done with smells and moisture, mouse droppings, rot. Electric is clean and dry; dust is its only negative.

For the interview, he sets up a time to meet at The Chili Hot, the largest and busiest of the three diners on Riverville's Main Street. They sit across from one another at a two-person booth, and when the startling blue of his eyes settle on Rubiat's face, Rubiat doesn't turn away. He looks at the craggy visage before him, the wild eyebrow hairs, the crooked, yellowed teeth, the cheeks mapped with veins. They have already exchanged a few pleasantries when Walter says, "What the hell, you're the only one to express an interest and I'm a desperate man, my knees are giving out. Let's say we sign a six-month contract. You move down here and give the job a whirl. That suit?"

It takes Rubiat by surprise. He's wearing a professionally ironed shirt, clean trousers and has tucked his long hair into a tight knot at the back of his head. He's boned up on the more obscure terms and routines for solving the rarer, more complicated problems. "The salary?" he asks. "Plus, I don't have tools or a van."

"That's the basic shape of it all. If you're in agreement, we can move on to details. Otherwise, it's a waste of time and breath. You're young, you don't have to think about these things, but when you're an old man like me, energy is precious. Now, let me tell you something. I'm not out to cheat you. You're going to charge the same hourly rate to customers that I do. Fair enough? My purpose is to help you succeed because your success ensures my success. Understand? You on board?"

Another opportunity to say yes. The ball was rolling along. "I like the town, from what I can see of it."

"Good. Now." Walter turns over the paper placemat and takes out a stubby pencil to write down details. "I got a van for you with a hundred and twenty thousand on the odometer. Good engine. Needs a muffler and if I know you're on board, I'll get it fixed. I charge thirty-five an hour. I recommend you charge the same. Everything you need is in that van. Hell, what am I going to do with plumbing tools? You rent the van and tools from me for six months and then we'll see."

"How much rent?" Rubiat asks.

"First things first. It's parked at my house. I'll take you over so you can see it. Then we'll talk."

Rubiat finds a place to live above the shoe store. The apartment has good light, a parking slot in back, and with the few things he's brought down from his rental in Rochester, it is a beginning.

In the evenings, he walks through the town. There are beautiful, big old Victorians built in the days the town supplied oil to the Northeast from its many wells, and there are sad, neglected ruins that have been divided into apartments. Everything is old. There is no new construction and the businesses on the outskirts, the gas stations, supermarkets, the few chain stores and restaurants, feel entirely separate. Riverville has been stubborn. In the face of commercial pressure, it has kept its soul.

There are two bars on Main Street, one at the eastern end where there is a roofing company, car dealership, and twenty-four-hour drugstore that sells beer, and the other at the more picturesque western end, close to his apartment. Called Lucky

Days, it serves a Friday fish fry, something he has discovered is popular in this area of the state.

On a Friday evening he walks into Lucky Days and orders a glass of soda water from the bar. When he sits down, he can feel the woman on the next stool turning to look at him, but he keeps his glance frontal, sips his water. If he were in a mood to be friendly, he would turn to her, but he's been busy, he's had at least five or six jobs to go to everyday, and he's tired of people. He wants simply to be somewhere besides his apartment, out in the public and yet alone.

"You're new here. Been seeing you around though. You work for Henry. I know he's been looking for somebody to take over the plumbing. That must be you, right?"

When he turns to engage, he finds a woman with frosted hair, decent cleavage, and long painted fingernails.

"Hey, don't look so surprised!" She laughs. "This here is small town life. Everybody knows everybody and their business." She has a practical face. It knows it's not pretty, but it accepts itself, and in the way she watches him, he can feel playfulness emanating from her tough, unlikely surfaces. "Sometimes it's too much, but in the beginning, it's just a way to be friendly." The conversation moves on from there and Rubiat is drawn into a game he's never played before as the woman leans in with increasingly intimate questions. Now why wasn't he with a girlfriend, a nice-looking man like him? And so young? Alone on a weekend? Well, she's alone too, but she has an excuse, she's married, and sometimes that's lonelier than being single. And how old would he be, if she could ask, that is? She's a decade older, a fact she announces outright. Truth to tell, she's getting tired of sitting on a bar stool. How would he like to meet up with her somewhere? She would leave first, he would wait ten minutes before he left, was that a plan? Under the bar, she slips him a piece of paper. He opens it on the sidewalk; it's the name and directions to a motel. She's attractive enough, but more than that, she's simply the next event in his life he's going to say yes to.

After that, they meet every few weekends, but despite a satisfying time together, their physical closeness doesn't allow talk. She's made it clear that anything outside of sex is off-limits.

Rubiat works long hours, often Saturdays too, and he drives many miles on small roads in the van he rents from Henry. He gets to know the land and the people, most of them are old and isolated, living out their years in the same houses they were born into. In the small towns radiating out from Riverville, more than half the stores on the main street are shuttered.

Walter Henry goes to The Chili Hot every day for lunch. He's often there for other meals as well, but Rubiat prefers to eat a simple dinner in his apartment. After a day of attending to customers, walking in and out of strangers' houses, he needs to be alone. But when his lunch overlaps with Henry's, he and the old man sit together. They talk about the jobs, but not in the ways Rubiat would have expected, not as partners with a common monetary interest. Walter doesn't seem to care about profit or loss, his concern is people, and since he has never lived anywhere else, he's known most of them all his life.

Rubiat fixed a leak under the kitchen sink in Mrs. Lamb's house in a far-away town. It was a small house with sloping floors and single-pane windows. She wore her coat indoors and sat in a chair near the heater vent in the living room, watching him with cold eyes. It was an easy fix. He saw the problem right away, but he didn't have the right size gasket. He stood up, his head brushing the ceiling. "Sorry, Mrs. Lamb, I'm going to have to order it and come back."

For a small, elderly woman, the power of her voice was startling. "And charge me for a second trip? Well, I may look helpless, but I'm not going to be cheated by someone less than half my age. You should have what I need. It's laziness and next time you can be sure I'm calling somebody else. Come in here! Let me see your face when I'm talking to you!"

He had been putting his tools away, and now he stood up, wiped his hands with the rag that hung on his belt, and entered the small, hot living room, filled with rugs and chairs, and the

La-Z-Boy she sat on, but no couch. He nodded his head toward her in deference, but also because the ceiling in the living room was lower.

"I don't like lazy men. You should know that. And look at you! No gumption, just a bag of too many bones. I don't care what you know, you're not going to take advantage of me. You get that, young man? And you tell your boss."

"We're partners," Rubiat said.

"Well then." She seemed flustered, but not enough to revise her idea of him. "What's your name?"

"Rubiat Elsayem, ma'am."

"What kind of a name is that?"

"It's an odd name I guess, but it's mine and I've gotten to like it."

"Good for you then, so when are you coming back?"

"End of the week. It'll take awhile to get the part. But you'll be okay till then. I've fixed it temporarily. But keep the bucket underneath just in case."

"That bucket's heavy when it fills up. Hard to get out the door."

"You don't have anybody here to help you?"

"If I need to, I can call my neighbor."

He knew there wasn't another house close by and driving there, he had noticed the miles of empty land. "Is there anything you need help with right now?"

"What do you mean?" she asked suspiciously.

"Something I could lift for you or fix for you?"

"No thank you," she said. "I get by on my own. I'm not helpless."

"I didn't think you were, but there's a lot of cold air coming in that front door. I can feel it. Let me look at it if I may."

"Suit yourself," she said, pulling her coat tighter, buttoning the top button.

When he returned with the new gasket, he also brought a roll of heavy-duty weather stripping and after fixing the leak in a permanent fashion he tackled the door. "She was so angry," he tells Walter, "that when I made the door snug she hardly acknowledged it. Not that it matters. I didn't expect gratitude, just maybe a grudging thanks. Do you know her?" Walter summons the waitress, orders another coffee. "Oh yes," he says. "Ada Lamb and I came up in school together." He spoons a teaspoon of sugar in his coffee. "Ada Lamb, she was angry then too. Her father left them high and dry, a mother, a few kids. Well, wouldn't you know it, she went ahead and married a man just like her father. Had one daughter who left for who knows where soon as she was old enough. That house has no TV and no couch because those are the tools of lazy men, drinkers like her husband and father, so she tossed them out. Her only book's probably the Bible, God knows what that woman does to pass the time. She's a tough one, oh yes, haven't seen her in years."

Walter shakes his head, stirs his coffee thoughtfully. "Yup, Ada Lamb. She's a hard, tough nut. I knew her when she was a bitty thing, thirteen, fourteen at most. Sassy and wild. We went swimming nekkid in the river. Never forget it. She was forward then. Liked to be naughty. Course, I liked it too. We said we'd marry and make it right. But I guess when time came, she was thick with someone else. Me? I was too tame for her, too tame by a long shot. And that's the long and short of it." Walter digs in his pocket for some bills, heads for the cash register. But when he returns to leave a tip he says, "You say you fixed her door?" He gives Rubiat a thumbs-up. "Good man. She's full of pride. Yup, full of sass even now. Wouldn't say thank you if you begged her."

23

When he first moved to Riverville he considered finding someone down there to talk to, but the idea of starting all over again with someone new felt impossible. He trusts Donna. He thinks she's a good therapist and he knows he's benefiting. He's crossed the threshold of a first plumbing hire and he hasn't been seized by impulse. Yet he doesn't altogether trust himself. He drives to Rochester every week for his appointment and though it takes extra time, he goes on the back roads, never the highway. So far, it seems as though he's not at risk. Still, he doesn't want to push his luck, and maybe the two-hour drive on slower roads helps. It's a preparation, a focusing, so when he enters her office he's ready.

"It happened in a split second. There wasn't even time to form the idea. I just did it, poof, I was in the air and then I was sliding down a vertical wall, fast, till I was stopped by a tree trunk, held in a thorny, spiky nest of branches. I wasn't there, really, I was in another space somewhere inside me. I think I lay in that nest for a long time. There was a helicopter, but I just stayed there, I couldn't move, I couldn't wave or stand up."

"I'm noticing your use of the word nest. Why would you call it a nest when it was full of thorns and spikes?"

"I don't know. It was a nest shape."

"Why do you think your mother never talked about your father? Especially considering that she gave you his last name. Might he have been around when you were born? Is that a fair supposition? Could we try it on, see what that feels like?"

"Sure, I'm game."

"And then, can we assume that he left her for whatever reason and so from an early time, maybe in your infancy, she was raising you alone. What do you think that felt like to her? How did that affect her and subsequently, how did it affect you?

When I say you, I don't mean *you* that you have a memory of, but an infant you, a pre-memory you. That's the mind, or consciousness we're after. What was your mother going through? You said she never spoke about your father, but was there anything that slipped, that might shed some light on the situation?"

Of course there was. And as the memory comes sliding back, he is amazed that he hasn't mentioned it. Or even realized it is significant.

The streets were slushy from the first December snow and there were icy puddles at every curb so by the time he got up to Lincoln Center his feet in his leaky boots were frozen. No one in the Elsinora family wore leaky footwear, but that Sunday Rubiat had pulled on his favorite broken-in and well-worn shoes. It was a small rebellion. He hadn't been in the store for over a year, hadn't wanted to be fit with the soft, glove-like boots and shoes they imported from Italy simply because...

Why? It was expensive, for one thing, not that anyone would have made him pay, but they *looked* expensive and were a sign of status he wanted to avoid. Nor did he want anyone in the family to make a fuss over his size thirteen feet, way bigger than his grandfather's or his uncle Matteo's. The last time they'd had to special order. The fuss of that alone was repugnant.

Socks wet, feet chilled, but it didn't matter. He was seventeen and forbade himself to notice. He owned a proper jacket but his uniform that year was a scarf and a blazer that he didn't bother to button. The one concession he made to winter was a pair of Italian leather gloves from the store, black, as soft as skin. He wanted to look windswept, impervious to cold, that was the image he wanted to create, and the form-fitting gloves were part of that, sexy and dangerous looking.

That week he'd received his driver's license and he was planning to get the car and go for a spin when his mother reminded him that Uncle Matteo had bought tickets for the opera and the plan was to meet in the lobby for the afternoon performance. She would have to miss it that year because his uncle wanted to have an outing with him alone. So Rubiat told the garage he wouldn't be getting the car after all and then he set out for the long walk up to Sixty-Sixth Street.

His uncle and his mother were the first generation who grew up speaking English, not Italian in the home. It was a hard-won Americanism that wiped out all traces of their parents' accent, but also made the rituals of their Italian heritage even more important. And that's why Italian opera and a meal at the city's most highly regarded Italian restaurant were an annual tradition. When he was younger, Rubiat had enjoyed it. But high school had lowered a fog of cynicism that made the experience suspect, imprinted as it was with his younger self. He could not take pleasure in something so upper-class and frivolous.

That year it was Rigoletto, a family favorite, but that year was the first time his mother wasn't sitting between them in the excellent seats Matteo always chose, her upright, correct posture an admonishment to Rubiat's slouch. Shoulder to shoulder with his uncle, a trim, gray-haired man who had stayed stubbornly single (rumors of lovers always circulating), was a pleasant change, and without her cloying perfume, his senses opened as the familiar story commenced. During the three hours, the voices on stage achieved such heights of tonal beauty his resistance was breached, and by the end, he knew he had experienced something vital. It was easy to stand next to his uncle, applauding till his palms felt numb and the lights came up. He was as excited, as grateful as everyone else. Like them, he had been lifted out of his life to experience something otherworldly.

As they walked across the plaza to the restaurant, they were silent. Speech, after such an extravagance, was wrong. It took all his will to keep the purity of those voices in his head and not allow the cold, gray city to take over. He wanted to lie down in his room and hear it all again in a more private way.

Instead, they arrived at the restaurant and that was when the trouble started. Matteo waited till they were seated in the hushed, carpeted dining room. Though it was December, management knew that any kind of music, but especially Christmas music, would be anathema to its many patrons coming from the opera. There was only ambient sound, the soft buzz of conversation, the clinking of silverware and dishes, all of it muted. When Matteo said, "Your mother is concerned about you, though perhaps you don't need me to tell you that. What bothers her is your lack—"

"I'm really tired of hearing about my lacks," Rubiat inserted, as the cloud of beauty lifted, leaving grimy, malicious life.

"Let me start again. We'll let your mother speak for herself when and if she wants to. The lack that concerns *me* is your lack of respect and honor for my sister."

"So that's why she's not here. The two of you planned this."

"No, not at all. It was my idea alone. It's past time you and I developed a relationship outside of your mother."

"But you're going to argue for her, aren't you?"

"This lack of respect," Matteo went on, ignoring Rubiat's comment, spreading the thick white napkin over his lap, taking a sip of the special wine he had ordered, the bottle sitting between them, candlelight reflected on its curved surface, "pains me terribly and it occurs to me that you don't know much of my sister's story and it is beyond time that you were apprised of some details. Beyond time for you to feel, how shall I put it, grateful, yes, grateful is the word for your mother's sacrifices."

They had ordered the cold antipasti and now there arrived oval plates of marinated vegetables, sliced red peppers, purple eggplant, broccolini, round plates of cheeses and meats, a basket of crusty garlic bread, navy beans gleaming under a slick of herbed oil with vinegary tomatoes arranged along the rim. At that age, Rubiat's hunger was desperate always and this bounty of food and drink was a practical way to ensure his presence. He was hungry also for attention from an older man. Matteo seemed to be volunteering for that part as well, and as he helped himself to a little bit of everything, filling his plate, his glass, dipping a slice of warm bread into a saucer of olive oil, he felt himself relax.

"We suspected that your father had a wife and children in

Morocco. A fact he kept from your mother who had been deeply in love with him and therefore, perhaps not the best judge
of character. You were a month old when he left. It was to be
only a few weeks, he told her, but he never returned, never
even contacted her and that, I believe, was his greatest cruelty.
To keep her waiting and hoping past, long past, the time any
reasonable person could be expected to wait."

"I don't even know his name."

"She called him Ahmed. Whether that was a nickname I
don't know. Ahmed. This is between you and me, Rubi. You
look like him. Tall and handsome, and I think you have his
restless nature. I can feel that, for instance, right now. He had,
and I think you have it too, a sense that this," Matteo spread
his arms out, indicating the room with the white tablecloths,
the well-dressed people, the waiters in white shirts walking
from the kitchen with plates balanced up their arms, "was not
good enough, would never even come close to his expectations.
He left her without anything. What would she have done if
we didn't have the store? Imagine her pain. A woman with a
month-old infant deserted by a man who simply disappeared.
Who never contacted her again, but who had made a promise.
Perhaps he had made it with no intention, from the beginning,
of ever returning. We don't know. Or perhaps events in Morocco prevented his return. Either way, nothing. A complete
vanishing.

"It was visible in her face. Such sorrow. But she had you.
You became her joy, her salvation, her reason for waking up in
the morning. She gave all her love to you. You are the central
figure of her life. You took away her pain. You were and are
loved and treasured and now it is time to pay some of that back.
It is the debt every child has to their mother, but yours, Rubi, is
larger than most."

He filled their glasses and made a toast. "To my sister, your
mother, Leona." Their glasses touched and they set about the
serious task of consuming the spread before them.

24

He took the car out the next day. He kept it all day, driving his friends from place to place, silly errands that would have been easier to accomplish by foot or subway. He showed off his parking skills, his knowledge of the traffic patterns in the densely populated neighborhoods of Manhattan. He took them up to Harlem where they ate dinner and went to a club, and after some drinks, they piled back in the car and he got on the FDR. It was two a.m. and it was around Sixty-Sixth Street when he had his impulse.

"So, what's the connection?" Donna asks. "Why then?"

"Lincoln Center, where we went for the opera, is at Sixty-Sixth Street, but that's just a coincidence. It was the first weekend I had my license, that's all. And I was busy showing off for my friends."

"Was anyone hurt?"

"No one, but the car was totaled."

"You like saying that, don't you? Totaled. Meaning destroyed. Was it like an expensive, fancy car?" Her hair is swept back from her face, the light illuminating her forehead. She seems unearthly, asexual, and though she is sitting some feet away, her voice is right outside his ear, close, focused.

"It was a silver beemer. An old model, by then, because we only used it in the summers, so it didn't have much mileage."

"You were underage. How did you get drinks?"

"Ah! That's something my uncle taught me. The art of the tip. A twenty-dollar bill discreetly passed from hand to hand."

"How did you feel afterward, after the shock of it had passed?"

"Really, really stupid. I wanted to dig a hole for myself and crawl inside."

"How could a car be totaled and no one inside it hurt?"

"It's just the word the insurance company used. It's totaled if the cost of fixing it is more than the car is worth."

"Whose car was it?"

"My mother's, of course. She loved it."

"Was she angry? Were you punished?"

"She was relieved no one was hurt."

"Right, of course. And the car? What was your conversation about the car?"

"I don't remember. I'm sure I said I was sorry."

"And were you? Because really, could you describe that accident as anything but reckless and defiant?"

"Stupid!"

"Right, it was stupid. But where did the impulse come from? What's the connection to your mother, is there one?"

"I don't know. My mother, when I think of her, represents safety, stability, nourishment, all the necessary things. She worked really hard and I know it was all for me. Aside from anger or frustration with something I was doing or saying maybe, I know she loves me."

"Okay, but I want to go beyond the obvious. Maybe it would help to go back to the day before. There you are experiencing this glorious, extravagant singing. It's so beautiful. Even the pain of the story. And then you go to the restaurant and Matteo fills you in on all the missing details. How did you feel after that?"

"Numb. I just felt numb. I walked the forty blocks back to our apartment and I ran a bath, fell asleep in the tub, and then I went to bed."

"Okay, numb. That doesn't tell us a whole lot. Can you be a bit more specific?"

"It's an impossible task. How can I repay a debt like that? I love my mother, of course I do, but…I don't know. It just seemed impossible. I wanted to run away from it. I wanted to disappoint her. I wanted to show her I wasn't who she thought I was. I was my father's son, I could vanish."

"Now we're getting somewhere. But wrecking her car isn't

vanishing. It's being even more present in her life. Am I right? Or did it mean something else to you?"

"I didn't intend to wreck her car. Isn't the hour up already?"

Her lips curl, her version of a smile. "Don't think about the time. Keep going. I've heard this before, haven't I? You didn't intend to dive off the cliff. You were only suggesting an absurdity."

"It just takes over," Rubiat says. "I have no control."

"Really? Is that true?"

"Yes, of course it's true!"

"Okay, then tell me what control feels like, when you have it, when it's working for you."

"It's like a part of me that tells me not to do something stupid, not to hurt someone else, not to hurt myself. It's the part of me that keeps me safe. And makes me want to protect others."

"It's reliable most of the time?"

"Yeah, seems to be. I mean, I'm not in the habit of doing crazy things, I'm responsible, dependable, all that stuff. I don't know why it deserts me occasionally. That's what I have to figure out."

"When it deserts you, what does that feel like? Does it feel very different?"

"It's like I'm raw, unprotected, totally full of rage. I want to wreck things. I want to disappear. I'm seized by impulse and I can't fight back. It's sick and I need help." He begins to cry. "I don't know what happens to me."

"How many people were in the car?"

"Four including me."

"As the driver, you are responsible for their lives. You could have killed everyone. How were you able to live with yourself after that? The car hardly matters next to the possibility of what might have happened. Four mothers might have lost their beloved children. Sons? Daughters? Were they all boys?"

"I know!" he shouted. "I get it! That's why I'm here! It was evil."

She looks at him squarely, her face neutral and bland. It's her voice that needles. "So, why'd you do it? I don't buy this 'I had no control crap.' You're not a cruel person. Where was your awareness at that moment?"

"We'd had a few drinks."

"No, that's the easy way out. I want you to go back there. Why'd you drive so fast you lost control of the car?"

"I wanted to fly. I wanted to not be human. I wanted to enter another dimension. I wanted to vanish myself, I don't know."

"Why would you want those things?"

"I wanted to not feel so much! I wanted to escape everything."

"What, specifically?" When he doesn't respond, she says it again. "What, specifically, did you want to escape?"

"I just wanted to live my own life. My own separate life apart from her and what I was required to be for her."

"And what was that?"

"The man in her life! It wasn't enough to be a son. I had to be the missing husband as well. I hate her! I hate all mothers. I can't be the one who gives her a reason for existing. I can't be my father!" He was on his feet, shouting, crying. "I can't do it. I can't do it. I can't be him!"

She doesn't say sit down, she looks up at him and waits.

"I can't live that way. They trapped me and that seemed like a way out. I would vanish myself."

"Go on," Donna says. "And the cliff? It wasn't absurdity, was it?"

"No, I was afraid of how deeply I felt. How she too would trap me. How she would want more than I could possibly give."

"Realizing that, what's your next step?"

"What do you mean?"

"How can you learn to trust that a woman won't ask too much? That another woman is not going to be like a mother who looks to you for all her emotional needs. How can you start to learn that? Let's begin there next week. Good work, Rubiat."

25

That evening, Matteo calls at ten o'clock, and without preamble, gets right to the point. This is how his uncle operates. He's willing to indulge in small talk with customers at the store, but family is different. With family, there is trust and love. It is always there, a foundation that was built a long time ago and always can be relied upon.

"A young woman named Rachel Goodwin came into the store. Do you know this person?"

Rubiat knows exactly where his uncle is sitting. He sees the gray walls, the antique fabrics on the carved wooden furniture in the living room that once had been in his grandparents' apartment several blocks south. Even though Matteo speaks on a cell phone he's sitting on the couch close to the end table where the phone used to be, his legs crossed, wearing a thick robe to cover his just-bathed body, thin hairy calves, long bare feet. It was a body he'd aspired to as a boy, though he has turned out to be thinner and taller.

Rubiat has also come from the shower and is standing wrapped in a towel, dripping on the linoleum floor that covers all three rooms of his apartment. He pulls on pajamas as they talk, then his jacket. Once the store below him has closed, the heat is minimal.

"From the art school," Rubiat says.

"She came into the store looking for you. I told Leona and she apparently met her for lunch, but she didn't give her your phone number. What would you like us to do?"

"What did she say?"

"She gave Leona the impression that she needed to speak to you, that it was urgent. And that the two of you had a strong bond. Leona said she was a bit hysterical."

"Hysterical? That doesn't sound like Rachel. How?"

"Well, it sounds quite unbelievable, really, but you know Leona. She doesn't misrepresent and she's certainly not prone to exaggeration. It seems she sang a song. Right there in the Macy's restaurant."

"A song?"

"Yes, apparently it was some kind of love song. Leona didn't know what it was. But it was a horrible spectacle. Very embarrassing for her. Actually, in truth, I think it sounds quite marvelous. She has the young woman's number if you'd care to contact her. I thought I'd let you know. Leona is against it. Finds her unstable. That's the situation."

They go on to other news and when the call ends, Rubiat sits at his kitchen table and looks at his spartan rooms. Nothing on the walls, nothing on the floors, the few pots and pans he has sitting on the stove. He doesn't own a computer. He works six days a week and the only person he speaks to regularly is Walter. It's pathetic.

And yet, it's a reasonable existence; he's worked hard to secure it. He remembers how Walter had talked about that woman, how his face had lit up with the memory. Does he want to be like him, a lonely man whose only love is in the past?

Still, he waits two days before calling his mother, fighting his desire for an uncomplicated life, a life with nothing more baffling than the problems of plumbing. Customers have learned they can rely on him and he's holding down his end of the business, maybe even growing it. It's sustainable. It could go on like this for years and then he's seventy, reminiscing about a wild time in his youth. That's what stops him. She had taken a chance. She had stood up in the middle of a restaurant and sang a song. The least he can do is call her.

When he dials his mother's number he knows exactly where the phone is ringing. The siblings share a love of routine, maybe it's something they have learned from running a business. He pictures her bedroom, the window opened two inches to let fresh air into the stale, overheated apartment. The kitchen sparkles with shiny saucepans hanging over the counter, the living room is a place of quiet and subdued light, rugs on the floor, plumped cushions on the couch, but she isn't in those places, nor is the phone. He dares his imagination to pass through the door of the bathroom where she lays in a tub filled with hot water to which bath salts have been added, a female figure lying prone, eyes closed but not asleep. He will not linger over her body, he will let the milky water shield it from his eyes. As her cell phone sounds, a wet arm comes out of the water and lifts a towel to rub between wet hands. "Hello? Rubi?"

She knows it's him without looking. No one else calls at that hour. They chat, each letting the sound of the other's voice calm them, hardly paying attention to what is said. It's simply the voice that matters. Slowly, he comes to the reason for the call and she says, "She's extremely immature and, personally, I don't think she would be good for you. But what do I know? I'll send you the number." His phone buzzes when the number comes through.

But when he calls the next morning he gets a recording for a construction business. Somewhere, a number has been changed. On purpose, he wonders, but decides it's simply an error. He will try her email. The next day he goes to the library and uses one of their computers to send a message: This is Rubiat. Please call me in the evening after seven p.m. Let's talk soon.

She doesn't call that evening or the next evening and the day after he is driving to Rochester for an appointment with Donna.

26

He steps into the muted light of the office. The blinds are drawn, the only light is the desk lamp, and Donna is wearing a gray, tent-like dress with a strand of pearls that draw his eyes to the prominent bones in her neck. He realizes she is older than he had assumed. There are no bright colors anywhere and as he sits down across from her, he feels as though his body is just as cleansed and neutral as everything else.

"Shall we begin with last week's question? How can you start to learn that another woman is not going to require you to supply all her emotional needs, that another woman will not be like your mother? How can you learn that?"

"That's why I have to follow-up on this other woman. I already sort of trust her, and I already made contact with her. The one who made me jump."

"If she's the one who made you jump, that doesn't sound like trust. Has something else happened since then?"

"Yes and no." He pauses. He isn't sure he wants to talk about it. "My mother met with her. I know that doesn't sound like an auspicious beginning, but my mother is very forceful. She wouldn't give her my email until they met. She wanted to check her out."

"Her? Let's dignify this woman with a name."

"Rachel."

"So your mother wanted to check Rachel out."

"Yes, odd and inappropriate as that is. My uncle, who is much more laid back than my mother, told me that in the middle of the restaurant Rachel stood up and sang a song. She did that strange, remarkable thing. She created a spectacle. It embarrassed my mother which I'm sure is exactly what Rachel intended. And then she simply walked out. So you see, Rachel has already helped me break away. By doing that. By not even trying to meet my mother's standards for good behavior." He laughs. And then he stops. He clears his throat. "The question is, will she be interested in me when she finds out what I've been doing? I don't think so. That's the part I'm dreading."

"Why?"

"She's very accomplished. She's an artist in New York City and here I am a plumber in a dead little western New York State town. She's not going to be interested."

"How do you know?"

"Look at me. I fix leaks."

"What's wrong with that? You do necessary, important work; people depend on you. And you're young, you're not bad looking." He has noticed that she avoids flattery. Not bad looking is as far as she will go, and in truth, the ambiguity of it comforts him.

"Look at my hands. They're permanently stained from grease. I crawl around in basements, I go where spiders go. It's filthy work."

"But it's necessary work. It's a skill, a craft. Are you good at it?"

"I am. But it's not so hard. There's nothing creative about it."

"It *is* creative and it *is* hard. It's problem solving. Why are you diminishing your ability? Look, you may not be right for one another, but shouldn't you at least find out if there's anything there? Instead of imagining how Rachel is going to see you, why don't you tell me why you want to contact her. You have a girlfriend now, right? What's going on with her?"

"Sex. That's the all of it. It's a thoroughly transactional relationship. I feel nothing for her personally. I enjoy her body. I think she enjoys mine."

"And you have no desire to explore more with her?"

"She's married. Sex is all she wants."

"I see. And given that, it surprises me that you would be dreading this contact. Wouldn't you like to have the possibility of an emotional involvement?"

"My fuck-buddy is safe. I won't drive too fast to escape impossible demands. I won't jump off a cliff. I don't know if I can handle emotions. I mean, I can handle emotions, but ones that are constrained, controlled, that have lines we can't cross."

"So what's the next step?"

"I sent Rachel my phone number. So now I'm just waiting. It's her move now. I'm sure she'll call soon."

27

Dusty finds a palatial apartment just five blocks from the co-op. It's the top two floors of a large stone house owned by a couple that occupies the first floor. His apartment gives him more space than he needs, but he hopes Rachel can be enticed to move to Philadelphia when she sees the huge space on the top floor, perfect for a studio, that he now uses for a bedroom because he likes the shower in the bath up there better than in the larger bathroom on the second floor where there is an eat-in kitchen, a living room, and a second bedroom that he uses as a study.

Never in his life has he had such elegant accommodations. The house features polished wood floors and antique fixtures. The generous porch at the front of the house has two doors; one is the entrance to his apartment on the upper floors and the other is the entrance to the owner's first floor residence. His door opens to a stairway leading up to a foyer that is the central hub of his apartment with the living room, kitchen, and stairs to the next floor coming into it. He luxuriates in the generosity of large rooms, in the fine architectural details that surround him.

But the job is not as trouble-free as he had been hoping or was led to believe. There is a staff member who has been there since its founding named Phillippa. Not only is she the bearer of history, she is viciously loyal to the founders. Most challenging is her proprietary attitude. It is her co-op and it has functioned until he arrived without major problems and she sees no reason for anything to change. Her resistance is fierce, yet she herself is a slight woman with short gray hair, delicate features, and a soft, flute-like voice.

Nine weeks into the job, Dusty proposes a new floor plan. He knows it's bold, but he also knows it will increase efficiency and shelf-space. He wants to move the two cashier stations to the back of the store where there is a small, never-used exit to the outside. He wants to enlarge it so there's a straight flow from front to back, rather than a circular flow that creates bottle necks at the front entrance on the weekends when the store is more crowded. Customers would come in the door on the street and exit at the back door. He figures the cost of the change would be no more than fifteen hundred dollars, the cost of installing a wider, heavier door at the exit, new locks, and re-building one wall. They could do the moving of shelves, counters, freezers, and refrigerated cases on a Sunday. Not only would the design improve the shopping experience, it would also make a statement that the co-op, under his leadership, would see innovation and upgrades.

He presents his proposal at a meeting of staff and board members when the azalea bushes and magnolia trees are in bloom along the street and the scents of blossoms sweeten the spring air. In front of the co-op daffodils and tulips are a cheery presence and the elm that spreads its generous bowers over all their comings and goings is furry with new leaves. Phillippa waits until the end of the session to raise her objections. Already, there have been questions and comments for more than an hour, and most seem cautiously in favor. Though their meetings are informal and no one bothers to raise a hand to speak, Phillippa stands up.

"Change is hard," she begins, "especially when the old ways have served us so well for so very long. So I will be devil's advocate because I am committed to the idea, if it ain't broke, don't fix it number one, and number two, don't let the glossy surface of the new and untried scramble your judgment. If you haven't heard of that second one, it's because I just made it up."

People laugh dutifully, but their faces show impatience. The meeting is dragging on and everyone wants to go home. Why didn't she voice her concerns earlier?

"I think turning the back door into an exit is a very bad idea. Here's why: You step out, it's raining, and suddenly buckets of water drench you and your groceries. There isn't a roof to protect you like there is in the front." She goes on to matters of security. She speaks softly and slowly, her reedy voice filling all the corners of the room, her body absolutely still because she never gestures as she speaks. She trusts her words to do their work. Her erect posture and precise features, her long chiseled nose and high cheekbones, her hard-as-ebony black eyes, under the thin arches of manicured eyebrows, make her persuasive. She is obviously not a sloppy person.

But she is wrong. It would be easy to make an overhang over that door, easy to make it work for egress only, and with the chaos caused by a narrow front door that is both entrance and exit, they will be more secure, not less.

But then comes the slap in the face. "With all due respect, I submit that Dusty hasn't been here long enough to understand all the ins and outs of our operation and all the many positives of our present, and I submit, appropriate floor plan."

The head of the board suggests they table the vote until the next meeting and take Phillippa's reservations under advisement.

Though the genders are equally represented on board and staff, Dusty notices that after the meeting, Phillippa is surrounded by women, while the men gather around him. They walk to the back of the store to look at the existing door and discuss details. They can hang a wider door without cutting through any beams, and a new metal door will be safer than the old wooden one. As the two groups start to leave, Dusty takes Aaron aside. Aaron is the board chair, a big, beefy man with a full beard and large belly that spills over his loose, well-worn jeans, a man who looks more like a lumberjack than a retired security systems analyst.

"What do you think?" he asks.

"The rose is beautiful, but it has sharp thorns," Aaron says softly. "Don't let her prick you. She's valuable as an antagonist because it makes us take a second look and question everything. That's good. Every organization needs an antagonist. But I know it can be unsettling. My advice? Don't make it personal. She has power."

"But a cooperative is a democratic institution."

"Even a democracy needs an antagonist. You'll see. You'll come to appreciate her. She has boundless energy. Meanwhile, I think your plan is a good one. But I want to sleep on it, talk it over a bit, try it out in my mind. Thanks for such a detailed, well-researched presentation." He gives Dusty a brotherly hand on the shoulder and walks out.

Dusty locks up. Then he walks home through the fragrant streets, but before climbing the steps to the porch, he sees her down the block and calls, "Phillippa!"

She turns around, but she doesn't wave, doesn't approach. She waits as he walks up to her, and when he's within talking distance she says, "It's a beautiful evening, isn't it?"

"I loved this neighborhood even before spring arrived, but now, with all the blooms it's even more beautiful. Is this where you live?" he asks, but realizes as soon as he's said it, the question is too personal. So he adds quickly, "I live in that house down there with the green trim."

"Right. I remember when those people applied for a zoning variance to add a rental space. I was against it. These old houses need our protection. I'm never in favor of cutting them up. Sorry to be so abrupt, but I have an early morning. Goodnight."

When he tries Rachel that evening she doesn't pick up and she doesn't try to catch him the next morning either.

28

The Chili Hot restaurant on Riverville's Main Street has been there since 1921. Their specialty, since its opening, is grilled hot dogs with a chili dressing served in a toasted bun. Walter Henry has a couple for lunch on most days, claiming that the tomatoes and peppers in the chili supply his daily vegetable.

"Yes, sir," he says, "you find you get most of your vitamins in condiments: ketchup, mustard, relish, things you take for granted. Cream in your coffee. That's your calcium right there. French fries. Greasier the better. That there is your fat and fat, contrary to what a lot of people think, is an important vitamin like all the others. Butter on your bread too. A body needs fat to function. Salt and sugar are necessary too. Balance. That's what it's all about." He pours a generous amount of creamer into his coffee and, looking at Rubiat's plate, which consists of a side of coleslaw and a side of home fries, the least objectionable items on the menu, says, "You're of a different opinion, I see. Well, here's to your health." They click cups.

They are sitting side by side at the counter because all the booths during the lunch rush are taken. "Heard something interesting the other day. Goes back to my story about the nekkid swimming. Poag's Hole. That land is for sale now. A phenomenon of nature and it's for sale. Just the five or so acres, but they contain the creek where the hole is."

Rubiat is only half listening to his lunch partner. Rachel still hasn't called, and it has been weeks since he sent the email. "What's Poag's Hole?"

"Hell if I know. It's a mystery is what it is. But kids been swimming there for ages and it seems a shame to put it up for sale."

"But why is it a mystery?"

Walter Henry turns to him and says, "It's one of the wonders of this nation, is what it is, and if not the nation, then the state, and if not the state, then the county. Definitely the county. It looks like any old creek you see anywhere. Rocks, a little bit of water, a pool here and there, little waterfalls here and there, little sluices. But then, all of the sudden, there's a hole under one of them waterfalls. And instead of water that comes up to your ankle, you are sucked all the way down, you are swallowed entire. No one knows how deep it is, but it's over your head, that's for sure. Way over your head. Why it's there and what made it, no one knows. How it was discovered. No one knows that either. But kids go there every summer. Word of mouth. Generation to generation."

"Where is it?" Rubiat asks.

"Few miles outside of town. Close. Easy drive. I'll show you sometime."

29

After three weeks not hearing from her, he goes back to the library and reserves an hour at a computer. By the end of that time, he has learned that she's been in several group shows and has even had a one-person show at a gallery called White Pillars. In addition, he discovers her website and so he sends a second email with the same message. This time, he knows it will reach her.

30

Five of the boxes are installed on the sixteenth floor of the Citibank headquarters in Manhattan. They are mounted behind a false wall, and all a person sees, as they walk down the hallway, are windows positioned at eye level. The first time Rachel goes in to view them she is disappointed, although everyone else gushes with excitement. They rave about the reactions of their clients, their staff, and visitors to the building. The gallery, of course, is very pleased and the check she receives is sizable.

But for her, they lack sharpness. She doesn't know how else to describe it. The first time a person views them they have a powerful effect. They invoke dream, folktale, myth, but with each subsequent viewing, the effect is blunted until finally, they are no different from billboards on the street, visual compositions passed every day that a person ignores. That's what happens with her boxes. It is only a matter of time before people walk past them, and even if they stop to look, they will no longer be able to see them in a raw and fresh way. How can she sustain the impact of the first viewing?

She keeps her disappointment to herself because she knows how lucky she is to get a sale like that. She doesn't even tell Angela and she never keeps anything from Angela. After the installation is completed, the gallery hosts an opening at Citibank, hoping to attract more collectors.

And many months later, a collector who had been to the White Pillars show and then saw the Citibank hallway does contact the gallery. He wants to commission her to make six boxes for his private museum. The gallery, of course, is thrilled, but it has been a year since Rachel has made any boxes. She's working on paintings now, yet the money is substantial and with the gallery involved, she can't turn it down if she wants to have a career. She bargains for a week and during that time she looks at her paintings and makes sketches of possible dioramas, incorporating elements she has been exploring in her two-dimensional work. The El series, the title she has given to her paintings, illustrate her search for a missing man. Except illustration is not the right word. Express, that's better. She wants to express the feeling of still not knowing, after all these years, what happened to him. Elsayem. With the stress on the last syllable, the name has a pleasing rhythm, while the first syllable of his first name is the one that gets stressed. Rubiat: it is a lasting, durable rhythm. She is haunted by the materiality of him, the sounds, images, sensations, and in the paintings, she has tried to make that very materiality vanish. She makes the E and the L insubstantial. They are already faded in some compositions, in the process of fading in others, and sometimes seem only to be smoke or vapor. She has tried to erase them by adding lines suggesting archways, subway tracks, windows, half-open doors. The canvases hold the tension between the known, the seen, the close-up versus the disappearing and far away.

Rubiat Elsayem: whether she says the words slowly or quickly, loudly or softly, he is still there, commanding a front-row seat in her memory. Maybe three dimensions will finally crowd him out, finally push him into the distance so that she can have her life back. At the end of the week she says yes to the commission and begins to sketch ideas. But then her intention changes. Working with true depth, not the implied depth of a flat surface, she understands that she cannot deny his presence; she cannot deny what he has done. The letters have a material structure. They exist, and she can't obscure them within the context of other shapes and lines. He exists somewhere in the world, and maybe a better intention is to bring him closer to her through the work. By degrees, she will inch the symbols of his name, an R, an E, an L, toward her in Queens. She will acknowledge his materiality; she will stop insisting on absence; she will face what he has done to her; she will look at it directly.

Immediately, the shapes of his initials seem more interesting.

She looks at illuminated manuscripts she finds at the Met and in rare books at the public library on Forty-Second Street, and though they illustrate religious texts, she is inspired by them. She wants to try to achieve a similar sense of something that is sacred, far beyond the ordinary. A person, someone she once knew.

The problem is that the deadline is only six months away. They must be finished in time for the grand opening of his collection. She will try to complete eight boxes, then choose the six strongest. It will take focus and concentration to finish in time, but she thinks she can do it. She will have to stop teaching and focus all her energies. No diversions or distractions allowed. She's been living with the moment he jumped off the cliff for so long it will feel like a freedom to finally admit it. When she hears her own scream over and over she won't allow herself to escape it, she will create actual three-dimensional spaces for it to live.

She starts to listen to the local news. It is a litany of accidents, murders, burglaries. She pays attention to the stories that involve a witness and it comes to her that the witness is a person with a peculiar burden, a twist of terror and powerlessness, a combination that produces psychic wounds that can never close. The boxes will be the testimony of all those unforgettable events, those nightmares of the unimaginable. They will show how the mind of the witness is drawn to that place, not to erase it—she has learned she will never succeed in doing that—but to acknowledge its importance.

She checks her email when she gets home and there, in the column of senders, she sees the very letters she has been working with, the R, the E, the L, shapes she knows intimately by now. Heart thumping like a rebel drummer, she double-clicks on the message.

But she doesn't read it. She closes his email, deciding to wait until she's made some dinner. Then she can read it while she eats. It is already ten p.m., and she has eaten only carrots and a handful of nuts since she left. She scrambles eggs, butters toast, whips up a salad, and sits at her small table with the food before her, looking into a diorama-in-process she hung on the wall opposite.

An R stands at the center, surrounded by shapes and colors that suggest leaves and branches. There are brilliantly colored and feathered bird-like forms perched on the top of the curve of the letter, and roosting in the branches around it. In the distance, an archway rises to the right of the R suggesting a farther, more hidden place with a shadowy, clouded R in its interior.

What would it be like to finish the box knowing all the particulars: where he's living, what he's doing, what happened after his dive into a rocky stream bed that anyone would have assumed caused death? The unknown would vanish, and as all the facts crowded her mind, the mystery that was the catalyst for the dioramas would disappear.

She opened her email and made a folder called "Read Later" and dragged his message into it. After five years, what would six more months matter? If her connection with him was truly as strong as it felt, then it would survive a delay. It might even get stronger. Right now, what she needed for herself was the gift of ignorance so she could imagine a world insulated from any news of the real.

But maybe that wasn't important. Maybe another mystery would take its place.

She looks at her empty plate, at her empty salad bowl, her empty water glass as the questions swirl in her mind. She runs a hot bath and instead of finding the answers, falls asleep. She wakes when the water turns cold, gets out of the tub forgetting to drain it, and stumbles into bed.

In the morning she knows with certainty she must go forward with her plan and that day in the studio she finishes the box she had brought home, painting over the R in the archway and filling it with darkness instead. She makes the remaining R more present, more alive, and with flashes of reds and blues she creates an unknown that has all the vibrancy and power she feels. She makes it beautiful.

31

Saturday. No plumbing emergencies in the three counties he serves. A blissfully empty day. Rubiat pulls into the driveway at Walter Henry's house and, keeping his motor running, runs up to the front door. The old man climbs into the van with a groan. "These old legs. Just wait till you're my age. Whole 'nother picture is what it is. Whole 'nother channel. Find yourself tuned into a horror movie is what it is. I promise you that." He snaps on his seatbelt and directs Rubiat to Poag's Hole.

"Now listen, it ain't going to look like much. You have to jump in to experience it. But at least you'll see where and you'll see the creek and the lay of the land and you'll know the place on the road where you have to park. Now, I ain't going to climb down there with you, I'll wait in the truck. You go see for yourself. I'll wait. You take your time."

With the van parked along the side of the road, the old man sitting in the cab, buttoned up in his coat because it's cold, Rubiat follows a well-worn path through bushes and trees to an opening where he can see a creek winding below him. He climbs down the bank, grabbing at weeds and saplings because the rocks are slippery with ice. The bushes glitter with frost. Chickadees zip from branch to branch, calling. Now that he's closer, he sees a cascade of icicles spilling from a little waterfall into the streambed. The path takes him to the edge and he steps onto a rock in the middle of a stream where a spit of water courses below ice. Under the icy falls there is a snow-brushed slab of thicker ice. He stamps on it with his foot, but it doesn't break. This had to be it. He steps onto it with all his weight and looks around. The land is wild and overgrown, but there are hills in the distance, maybe even fields.

When he climbs back to the truck Henry says, "What'd you think?"

"It intrigues me. Who's handling it, do you know?"

"Oh, you don't want to mess with that. You'd have trespassers all summer long. Don't be a fool, boy. There's no way you could keep people off."

"No, I'm interested."

"What the hell for? Your own private diving spot?"

"That's exactly why I want it."

"Get out! That's the most foolish thing I ever heard. But it's Victor Properties. Something tells me you might already know her." Walter smiles, then adds, "But I keep that to myself because I like you, Rubiat. Here's a warning: Shaun Victor is not someone you want to cross. Not in this town. You hear me?"

"Thank you, I did. But how did you know? We've been so discreet."

"Let me tell you something. A small town is a public place. Everybody knows everything. And you, being a new person, a conspicuous person I might add, are an interesting subject to the rumormongers. Never doubt it."

Rubiat drives back on Sunday and walks the area around Poag's Hole. Down a bit from the stream he finds an old driveway and the remains of a foundation and a chimney. There are lilac bushes covered with buds and what might be peony bushes next to old slabs of concrete that must have been a sidewalk up to a long-vanished house. There is a willow nearby, and the creek, curving away from the place where a house once stood, looks like an ordinary creek, no deeper than any others. Why did that particular waterfall drill down like that? Maybe the stream bed, in that one spot, had an underground channel, or some sort of glacial chasm.

He remembers something Denton said to them long ago, in the class on performance art. An artist never acts on his own impulse alone. An artist is an instrument that receives input from the outside world. You are the landscape, the social context, the political context, and the generational era.

"You are the landscape." The way the ancient driveway curves down toward the missing house, the way the land flattens out around the creek and up to the distant hills gives the property a private vista. But the Hole is the center, the energy, the source. He can feel it calling him.

Just before he walks away, he sees a hawk sitting at the end of a branch high up in a tree. It isn't looking at him. He is irrelevant. Its head is turned toward the creek, and then it glides down silently on spread wings, its tail like an opened fan, the color red catching the afternoon light as it swoops over an unlucky rodent.

32

I'm surprised you know about it," Linda Victor says, sitting on the side of the bed at the Vista Vue Motel, fifteen miles away from Riverville in the next county. They've had a morning of leisurely sex, old lovers now, comfortable with one another. "We haven't listed it yet." She pulls pantyhose up her legs. "Oh, I know who. Walter Henry. He knows everything. He probably knows about us. That man's ears are satellite dishes, every little tremor gets picked up."

Rubiat is naked, lying on top of the bed, his cock flaccid now, resting across his thigh. "He'll be circumspect. I wouldn't worry."

They always arrive and depart separately. The owner is an old friend of Linda's who lets her park behind the building. That afternoon, Linda and her husband are going to drive to Toronto to see a Broadway play.

"In Toronto?"

"Why not? It's a real Broadway play and if I don't do these things with him he gets suspicious. It's my wifely duty."

"Linda. How much is it?"

"God knows. He got the tickets."

"The land."

"Oh, ten. Two thousand an acre. It's not good for anything but there's road access. Used to be a house even."

"Why's someone selling it?"

"Money. Why else? Acreage has never been this high before." She glances at herself in the mirror, then bends down to kiss him goodbye. The door clicks shut, and he hears the sound of her car pulling around on the gravel.

The time alone in a motel room after Linda leaves is the strangest time he has ever spent, absence scrawled in the ironed sheets of the rumpled bed. Rubiat stays on top of the bed watching the room ignore him, feeling the minutes accumulate. It is an in-between period, an exquisite suspension of activity, and sometimes he stays there for half an hour, savoring it. He doesn't have ten thousand dollars, but already, he feels as though the land belongs to him. And that's odd. He's never thought of settling in Riverville. It's only the stopping point on the way to somewhere else. But she hasn't called. He knows he has no right to expect anything different, but it surprises him that a woman who stood up to sing a love song in a crowded restaurant wouldn't even return his email.

33

The house sits below the road and is approached by a driveway that makes an elegant descending curve just like at the Poag's Hole property. The porch is an apron around three sides and Rubiat can tell it was a later addition to what must have been a stark, uninteresting exterior.

"The sump pump runs all the time," Solomon Vetterman says, taking Rubiat down a set of stairs, turning on lights as they descend into an underground that has a surprising amount of daylight, "and so far, it's able to keep up with the moisture, but I dread to think what's going to happen when the snow melts. It's our first winter in this godforsaken climate, and as a homeowner, I'm starting to understand the challenges of a northern winter." He's thin and tall like Rubiat, but his bones are prominent, and his face, neck, and shoulders have a knobby appearance that his hooded blue eyes and nervous laugh only accentuate. He is as ungainly and awkward as a teenager, yet he's a professor at the art school. "What do you teach?" Rubiat asks as the two men walk the perimeter of the basement, Solomon in rubber boots, Rubiat in his heavy workman's shoes. There aren't puddles, but the floor is wet and the sump pump chugs steadily.

"Art history," Solomon says. "This is a new furnace, new hot water heater, but everything's going to rust from moisture. I don't know what to do short of moving the house. I worry about mold. Is the furnace blowing mold into the rest of the house? It just doesn't seem very healthy. But it's probably been like this for eighty years. Any ideas?"

The basement has an unusually high ceiling. Rubiat usually has to stoop under pipes and heating ducts, but in this house they're over his head. He feels the walls, turns on his flashlight and examines them. "There's no mushrooms, no moss, no sign of mold that I can see, and the walls are dry. Do you keep the windows open?"

"Didn't want to introduce any more cold. You know, not when I'm heating with propane that costs two-fifty a gallon. I want the basement to be as warm as possible. The furnace vents down here, so that's good. I was even wondering if I should lay a new concrete floor and make a ditch that runs along the edge and spills out through some kind of a gutter. But then you'd have to do a slope to make the water exit, which means the floor would be angled, not flat."

Rubiat runs his light over the wooden beams holding up the first floor. He feels the undersides. There isn't any sign of damp. He looks at the basement windows, all of them, he can see now, dusty and tightly closed, are unusually tall and he says, "Either the person who built this house didn't want to stoop in the basement, or, and this is what I think, he knew that he was building in a wet area and so he gave the basement a high ceiling so there would be good air circulation, and he made the windows tall so there would be plenty of light, and in the summer they could be opened to get some airflow when the furnace was off. I think he figured the sump pump would be able to handle the water and was willing to accept that. The short and the long of it"—this is a phrase his partner uses all the time—"is that you don't have a problem. Whoever designed this house knew what he was doing."

Solomon laughs. "You're kidding!"

"You'll probably have to replace the pump every five years but they're not expensive. You just have to make sure it's always working. Clean and lubricate it every season, that sort of thing." He follows Solomon back up the stairs.

"Well, you came all the way over here from Riverville and I want to pay you for that, but can I offer you a cup of coffee?"

"Sure," Rubiat says, "let me take off these wet shoes."

Solomon stacks papers and books that are spread across the kitchen table. He sets down two cups. "Ever hear of this?" He holds up a large book called *Falling Water*.

"Falling water, what an interesting phrase."

"It's a house outside of Pittsburgh built over a stream by a famous architect. Maybe you've heard of him, Frank Lloyd Wright?"

"I have," Rubiat says. "I went to Crandall for a semester. Took art history even. But no mention of Falling Water that I recall. I think I would have remembered it."

"When was that?"

"Feels like ages ago, but it's been four, five years. The house is built over a stream, you say. Can I see?"

"It's a marvelous place. I go every summer. It's made up of cantilevered levels," Solomon says, pushing the book toward the plumber. "And the curious thing, that is, the most curious about a building that is so exquisitely situated into the woods around it, is that from the living room you can walk down a set of stairs," Solomon turns the pages, looking for a particular photograph, "here they are, there's this little gateway, see, right in the living room, and it goes down to the stream that runs below the house. It's not just that he built it on wet, unstable ground with a perpetual wet basement like this place, he went further than that, he actually brought the stream into the interior. That's what I love. He welcomed it."

"I see why you were attracted to this place then."

"Common sense would be to shut it out. Not invite all the problems water introduces into a house. But he created this little doorway to it, this little peek."

Rubiat was flipping through the photographs. "I have to see this place. It's open for tours?"

"Not in the winter," Solomon says. His eyes, face, hair reflect the light from the window and his thin fingers holding a pen tap on the table impatiently. He laughs with a short bark. "Sorry, I just stopped smoking. I'm fidgety. I would give anything to have a cig but I promised Edith, that's my wife. So I tap a pen, jiggle my knee. Do you smoke?"

"Never started."

"It's a wonderful habit, punctuates time, gives empty fingers something to hold, needy lips something to grab. I never realized how restless I am." He looks at Rubiat and says, "So if I can ask, how did you get from art school to plumbing? I assume you're from around here?"

"Attraction to water, I guess. I grew up in Manhattan."

"An island boy! I am too. Bainbridge Island off Washington State. Falling Water opens on April first. Shall we go together? Edith is tired of it. I could call you."

34

Driving back, he sees her car parked in front of the real estate office and pulls in next to it. She looks officious sitting behind the desk. Absurdly proper. She's clearly displeased when she sees him. "He's going to be back in ten minutes. We can't do this."

"It's real estate business. I'm here about that land."

"The land?" She is struggling to integrate the separate compartments of her life, and he watches as she casts back to their last morning at the motel. "Oh, right, Poag's Hole."

"Yeah, how could I get a loan?"

He had always assumed she was good at her job and so her efficiency isn't a surprise. She writes a name on a pad and hands him the sheet. "There's a bank in Canisteo. Right on Main Street at the light. You can't miss it. This is who you want to talk to."

They don't touch, they don't speak of other things, they don't even acknowledge anything with a secret look, and when he walks out of the office and sees her husband drive up, he understands her methods. She is a pro at this; she knows how guilt stains the expression if there isn't time to remove it. Rubiat tries not to stare, as the man he assumes is Shaun Victor, bends to get out from a low gray sedan. He's big, with thick arms and shoulders, but as he walks to the front door of the building, he moves like a man who at one time had been an athlete and still assumes he has that special distinction. His muscles will never be flab and Rubiat suspects he works out, less to maintain, more to threaten.

35

When he was ten years old, his mother took him to the neighborhood Y for swimming lessons. She watched from the bleachers as he and all the other children in his class dove off the concrete edge into the pool. The diving board would come later. They popped off, one after another, skinny boys and girls in wet bathing suits, shivering in the cold air, doing what they were told. They put their toes over the worn, paint-faded edge, raised their arms over their heads, hands pointed and touching, and fell in. Half of them did belly smacks. When it came to Rubiat's turn he took his time and in his mind he made a great leap and knifed into the water silently, going down and down, deeper than he had ever been before until, magically, he rose back to the surface. He wasn't scared at all. Rather, he was exhilarated to be able to go from the dry world of his mother to a hidden wet place.

After he finished the basic course, he started going to the free swims. He spent all his time diving off the edge just to experience that moment when he vanished from sight. He learned to delay the popping back to the surface as long as possible, training himself to hold his breath underwater. Stroking back to the ladder to climb out of the pool, he felt as sleek and water darkened as the fish he saw laid out on ice at the fish market.

He was curious about the diving board. He wandered down to the other pool and watched until he felt confident enough to try it himself. The first time he jumped off, he discovered the third element: sky. He went from human, to bird, to fish, and the moment he vanished into the water was a completion of the cycle. Bird was his new identity. He didn't care for swimming, had no interest in laps or water games. He went straight to the diving pool and spent all his time there, popping off the board over and over. He was eleven by then and he didn't care about form or technique. He didn't know the names of the different dives and there wasn't a way to learn them because diving classes started at age sixteen. All he wanted was the sensation of going from ground to sky to water. He jumped on the board as hard as he could to rise into the air as high as possible, and then he bent over, head tucked in, arms leading, to enter the water and travel all the way down to the soft and forgiving bottom of the concrete pool.

On some afternoons there was an older boy he'd noticed before. He had a trim muscled chest, and he performed the kind of dives you could see on television. Sometimes he was there with a man who seemed to be his teacher. But on the day he spoke to Rubiat, he was alone, and they were the only ones in the diving pool.

"You're doing it all wrong. Did you know that?"

The tiled walls broadcast sound, but Rubiat was so submerged in private sensations he didn't realize the boy was talking to him.

"Hey you! Didn't you hear me? You're doing it all wrong."

"I don't care," Rubiat shouted, trying to ignore him.

"Well, I could show you a few things, that's all. Like, your feet have to be together."

"So what!"

"And you have to know the dive you're going to do before you leave the board. You have to prepare for a specific dive. Get it?"

"So what!" Rubiat said again. He climbed out and headed to the locker room. It was ruined.

But the boy came in when Rubiat was getting dressed. "Didn't mean to offend you or anything. What's your name? I'm Devon."

"Rubiat," he answered softly.

"What's that?"

He took a breath to fuel his courage and said, "I don't want to tell you my name."

"It was Rube or something. I'll call you Rube. I think you

have potential, Rube. To be a good diver, I mean, and I could help you."

"No thank you," Rubiat said. He dumped his wet trunks into his backpack, not taking the time to put them or his wet towel in the plastic bag his mother gave him every morning. He hoisted his pack onto his shoulders and left.

"Bye-bye, Rube, see you later."

He stayed away from the pool for a week, but then he couldn't stand it any longer and went back. There was the familiar assortment of nondescript people, ugly men and women in ill-fitting suits who minded their own business as before. No Devon in sight. He could once again enter the cycle, boy, bird, fish, with no one watching.

36

A t the next session with Donna he tells her all of this and when he's finished she says, "Very interesting. Tell me more. Did you ever do diving seriously?"

"In high school I started to learn the right way to do it and I was on the school team, but I wasn't very good at it. Even then, I didn't really care about technique. It was the other things, even then, that compelled me."

"Why? Do you know why?"

"I have no idea."

"Did you ever want to learn scuba diving? Stay underwater for a really long time?"

"No, too much fuss, too much equipment. It wasn't being underwater so much as traveling from one state to another. That moment lifting off, that moment splashing into. I don't know why I was so enamored of that. It was like going through one door, then another door, then a third."

"Do you do it now? Do you go to a pool and dive?"

"No, I haven't been in a long time."

"Do you want to?"

"Not really. It doesn't seem so important now. Maybe being an adult I don't feel the same magic." But then he flashes on Poag's Hole and says, "I'm trying to buy a piece of land. Just five acres, that's all I can afford. But someday I'd like to build something." He doesn't tell her about the hole, and he wonders why. He doesn't want to admit to buying something just on hearsay. Even if he manages to get a loan, it will be months before it's warm enough to experience the hole himself.

"So you think you might stay there then?"

"I guess I'm thinking that, yes."

"How does it feel to say that?"

"Difficult, scary. But I need something to look forward to. It feels empty now. Rachel never called or answered my email and I think I have to give up on her. I have to create my own life. I also think I have to end things with Linda. But I can't until I get that land. She's the agent for it, but we're kind of drifting apart anyway. I think it's just going to fizzle out on its own."

"That all sounds really good, Rubiat. Actually, you're doing so well I don't think you need to continue to see me once a week. Do you agree?"

"Yeah, I was kind of thinking that too."

"We could go to once a month or we could say, make an appointment when you need to talk. It's up to you. A monthly appointment?"

"No, I'm good. Thank you for everything. You've been extremely helpful."

They shake hands. But then she steps closer and gives him a hug.

As he walks to the van he smells the fragrance of her skin, sees her glistening, damp eyes, and wonders, again, what the sadness is in her life.

37

The boxes sit on a wide shelf set shoulder height along a wall of her studio. There are six, each with the same elements: the letters R and EL, the curved lines, and a sense of distance that is created by many layers in shades of blue, gray, and purple with hints of other, more brilliant colors. The windows at the front of the boxes are rectangular. They are all the same size, but the hidden light source in the interiors is positioned in different places so the lighting changes from box to box. She wants the interiors to be a magnet for attention; she wants the illusion of distance to work. She wants to convey the sense that there is something precious at the end of the eye's journey. Sometimes it is the letters themselves, sometimes it is only a hint of the letters with a more beguiling mystery behind them. The problem is that she has lived with them for so long, putting them together piece by piece, she can't tell anymore if they create the desired effect. She needs an outside opinion.

Dusty has been hinting that he wants to come for a visit but she doesn't think she can trust him to tell the truth. She needs to find someone who will have a truly objective eye, someone who doesn't want anything from her. She doesn't want the woman at the gallery to see them either, at least not yet. She needs to know, first, that they are working. Maybe Angela? But she is a friend, which means she is already predisposed to like them. She needs someone who doesn't know her, someone completely uninvolved in her life. She isn't sure how to find such a person but that evening, when she's locking up to leave, the man who has the studio across from her is locking his door as well. They have never spoken, but Rachel has seen him before.

"Hi."

He turns around in surprise. "Oh, hi there." He's dressed in work clothes and has the casual, friendly bearing of most people her age who live in the city. "Would you happen to have a few spare minutes to come into my studio to look at something? I'm Rachel, by the way. I know this is awkward, but are you in a rush?"

He's holding a cardboard box full of vegetables and sets it down. "Arthur," he says. When they shake hands, she notices how dry his palms are. From acrylics? Is he a painter too?

"I need someone to look at what I've been doing. Would you have fifteen or so minutes? I don't think it would take very long."

"Sure thing. I guess I can leave this here. Who's going to want a box of celery, right?"

She takes him into her space and switches on her boxes. "I'm not going to say anything. I just want you to look and sort of, if you can, describe what you see. Or describe, if you could, the effect of what you see."

"Happy to," he says, and he walks, slowly, from box to box. She watches his back; he wears a shapeless brown jacket and an orange knit hat. He's stuffed his gloves into his pockets and they hang out like wings. His shoes are sturdy and well-worn; the first thing she noticed about them were the bright red laces. He's taking his time, moving from box to box silently. She gets a broom and starts sweeping under her worktable. She wants to give him space.

She's at the other end of her studio when he says, "Okay, I'm done."

But then he doesn't say anything and she has a terrible sinking feeling. He was the wrong person completely, or he is so unmoved he's trying to figure out how to lie about it. She notices his wide jaw, his dark brown eyes, and then his stubbly cheeks and as she's looking, they start to melt. He's trying not to cry. "Oh shit," he says, pulling a filthy-looking handkerchief from his pocket. "Sorry. My sister died three weeks ago and I'm still kind of vulnerable and I guess…it's just, I was looking into this better place, over and over, and it made me feel like I was seeing where she had ended up. Her soul, really. I was seeing it find its way, over and over. It was…intense I guess is the word. Sorry. This is probably not what you wanted. She was my older sister and she took care of me. Her soul is here. That's what these very beautiful constructions are telling me. Her soul is in the embrace of the universe, in the ether, if you know what I mean, and it's comforting to have it represented visually. That's what I'm getting here. I hope this makes sense. I know it's not what you wanted, probably, but I've got to get going. I'm part of the chicken soup project and they need my celery. They're serving in three hours. It's empty bowls, do you know about that movement? It's good to meet you, Rachel." He holds out his hand and when she takes it, she sees his mouth quiver again. "Thank you for having me in. They're really powerful, as you can tell. Can we talk later? I really have to get going."

She finishes sweeping the floor, and then she locks up for the second time. But she stops on the landing to gaze into the night sky. It is a deep navy, pillowy and thick, and the headlights of passing cars define the length of the street which stretches all the way out to a distant blur of neon that is the center of Long Island City. Below her are the perfect green globes marking the entrance to the subway. She's filled with happiness. Now she knows the title: *Night Journey one through six*.

38

He begins to see her everywhere, at the gas station, the liquor store, on the street, often at the co-op where she does little more than nod hello. She dresses in black. It's dramatic against her short silver hair and her tense, thin body. She seems starved and anti-female. He calls her "the bat," but only to himself. He wishes he had a friend he could joke around with, and wonders if the couple who own the house know her. When he sees Hugh on the porch one evening, he asks in as casual a tone as possible, but Hugh surprises him.

"The horror of Phillippa Drury," he replies. "Yes, well, we told ourselves it wouldn't be long!" Hugh is a classic kind of guy, always well-dressed, polite and friendly, but exceedingly formal in manner. He's tall and from his great height he exudes benevolence. "I don't envy you at the co-op. She runs this neighborhood like it's her private kingdom. She owns its history and thinks that gives her a right to claim its future. These old houses are too big to take care of and too expensive to heat. They will survive and the neighborhood will thrive only if they can be broken up into rental units. It seems obvious to everyone else but her. People don't live with extended families anymore. They don't have servants. They can't afford so much space. But she lobbied against it, marshaling all her connections. It passed, the zoning modification that allowed your apartment, but just barely. We wouldn't have been able to stay here if we didn't have a rental space. How is it working out for you, by the way?"

"Well, except for Phillippa, I love it. I'm hoping my girlfriend will come down. She's in New York paying lots of rent and I think she's going to fall in love with this place when she sees it."

He has put it off, waiting till he's more settled, and then one evening he knows he's ready. The Buddhist Center is downtown, and he has discovered he can get there on the commuter train. He begins to go every week, but it's still unsettling to have the familiar routine, yet be among strangers. He usually goes on Monday evening, but then he tries a Friday evening meeting as well. He doesn't have a social life, his nights are free, and he figures he might as well. But Friday nights, he sees right away, are attended mostly by the older members of the Sangha.

On the third Friday he recognizes some of the faces. As he takes his coat and shoes off in the hallway outside the large meeting room he can tell it's more crowded just by the jumble of outerwear and when he steps through the heavy velvet curtains into a warm, softly lit space where the people who can manage the floor are seated on cushions, and the ones who can't (only five), sit on chairs in the back, the murmur of foreign sounds, as people hold beads in their hands, counting mantras, is especially reverberant. No one takes notice of his entrance. He chooses a pillow and goes to the outer edge of the room and soon he's copying the posture: back straight, beads to chest, lips moving as his voice joins the others in the room. He keeps his eyes on the front of the room where the altar, a cloth-covered table with a statue of the Buddha and bowls of offerings sit, flanked by the graying heads of the elders in the community. Phillippa. She occupies the last cushion in the first row and if he listens closely, he can detect the fluty tones of her voice in the general hum.

A bandit. When a raccoon got into the chicken house, his father shot the raccoon. But when a hawk went after the chicks, carrying them off, one by one, he built a run that had a roof over it. It kept the hawk out, but the chickens could no longer wander, and they soon stripped the ground in their enclosure of every blade of green. It didn't make sense to raise chickens on starved brown earth. So his father dismantled it and they learned to live with the hawk's predations.

Here he was, sitting cross-legged on a red cushion in a house in Center City Philadelphia thinking about chickens as he intoned Tibetan words he didn't understand and watched the straight back of a woman in the front row. Why was it that in his lonely life in this new place the person who kept popping up was his enemy?

At the end of the meeting, everyone shakes hands and introduces themselves, and as the two people who are sitting on either side of him chat, they seem to know each other, he stands up and heads to the hallway wishing that he, too, had someone to talk with. He remembers this desperately lonely feeling from grade school when he asked the first person he knew was in his grade: Will you be my friend? He said yes and they were friends for years. A man is putting on his coat and says, "Can I give you a lift, Phillippa?"

"I'm taking the train, thank you."

"I'll drop you off at the station."

"Oh no, that's very kind, but it's out of your way. I'm fine walking."

"It's a dark night. You're sure?"

Dusty pipes up. "If you're walking to Suburban Station, I'll join you."

Phillippa hadn't seen him until then and when she realizes who it is she laughs. "We're neighbors," she says to the man who had offered a ride. "We'll walk together."

And that's all it takes before he's step to step with the woman who haunts his waking life. They talk about the Center and he tells her about the dharma house he had lived in in Brooklyn.

"You must have been sorry to leave it," she says.

"I was. I also left my girlfriend, but I'm hoping she'll move to Philadelphia. I just have to get her to come for a visit. She's an artist and she's been really busy with a show and then a commission, and I know she'll fall in love with our neighborhood. Everyone who lives in New York, they're starved for space and it's so available here. It's really quite amazing."

"We do get a lot of people escaping the high rents. It's one of the perks of our city. You're liking it here then?"

"I love it," he says with an enthusiasm he isn't sure he feels.

"Glad to hear it."

He likes walking with her. Their strides are the same length and they're lock step from the beginning. On the platform they wait side by side and continue to talk.

"It's been lonely though. I miss my girlfriend, like I said, and I miss friends in general. You've probably lived here your whole life."

"You're right. I've never had to move. I've never had to go through that."

"Can I ask you something?"

She looks surprised, her face alert and watchful. That's when he knows he's the baby chick; just because they're standing side by side he shouldn't be fooled. So, he doesn't ask the existential question, is that why you oppose change, and says instead, "Who planted the flowers in front of the co-op? I've always wondered."

One day his father stopped at the dog catcher's and brought home a scruffy brown mutt named Buster. He immediately chased down a chicken and killed it, but before he could start eating it, his father took the carcass, sprinkled it with a thick coating of cayenne pepper, and left it in the yard for the dog to find. It took only one taste. After that, he knew chickens would give him burning mouth. For all the years they had him, he protected the poultry, and the predators around their farm, the raccoons, foxes, and weasels, knew to stay away.

Dusty asks at the co-op if there's anyone who wants to give away a dog. He tells Hugh he'd like to get a dog and wonders if they would mind. Hugh says he hopes he'll get an older, quiet dog, not a puppy, and directs him to the animal shelter. But all they have there are puppies, yappy and excited, trying to burst from their cages as he follows the attendant down the concrete walkway.

"Any of them catch your fancy?"

"Actually, what I'm looking for is an older dog. An already house-trained, quiet, older dog."

The man leaves the building without a word, and Dusty

doesn't know if they're finished, so he waits in the foyer where the odor of a chemical cleaner assaults his nose. He's pathetic, a man looking for friendship from a dog. A dog would make it impossible to go to New York to visit Rachel. He's surprised he hadn't realized that earlier, but just as he's walking to his car, the man returns. At his side is a small, scruffy shepherd-like dog, exactly like Buster. "This is Macy. He's been living with us for a few months and I can attest to his good manners and quiet nature. He's fixed; he's up to date on his shots, and if you can make a donation, because donations are how we survive, he's yours. Someone brought him in, oh, about six months ago. He'd been living on garbage, who knows for how long, and the dog catcher was after him. My kids named him Macy and it sort of fits. I recommend you stick with it because this dog's been through a lot. If you think you can give him a stable, secure home he's yours. We got pretty fond of him, but we have six others, and my wife is tearing out her hair."

Dusty kneels to look in the dog's face. Round, red-rimmed eyes full of the very same sadness he's been feeling himself. How could he promise this animal anything? "I better not," he hears himself saying, but he's still on his knees. The dog lifts a forepaw and places it on his thigh, keeping him there, red eyes lifted to his face, the short black nose butting his hand.

"I think he wants to go home with you," the man says. "Are you sure?"

"I don't know." He asks the dog, "What do you think?" and the dog yawns and settles himself more comfortably.

At the supermarket Dusty buys dog supplies. He creates a spot in the kitchen for the animal's bowls and a corner in the bedroom for his bed. Macy inspects the rooms, wagging his tail and sniffing at all the corners. And that evening, when Dusty is meditating, he curls up next to him.

Over the next days he learns that Macy is agreeable with most things. He especially likes hearing Dusty sing, but second best is conversation with Dusty in which the dog is an attentive listener. He is always agreeable to a walk, but once he follows

Dusty down the stairs and out the front door, he insists on going left. Twice a day Dusty passes Phillippa's house. He learns to recognize her car and notes the presence of visitors, signaled by other cars in her driveway as well as more lights. He feels like a jealous lover.

But left also takes them to a small park and a chance for Macy to run. Though often, once the leash is unclipped, Macy prefers not to. He prefers to stay at Dusty's side as they pass under the trees, a mixture of elms and oaks, an especially tall American elm that Macy always lifts his leg at. It has wide, curving branches and Dusty begins to notice its power. This is what he's been missing and he thanks Macy for leading him toward it. The dog hears, gives a tail wag, but he keeps his nose on business, tracking scents left by previous visitors.

In the foggy distance Dusty sees someone else walking a dog. She wears a long silver coat and like him, she's looking up into trees.

39

Rubiat likes the simplicity of Riverville. It has one commercial street, not even a mile long, and its three busiest blocks include The Chili Hot, a shoe store, a hardware store, three hairdressers, and a large library housed in a classical building that also contains a community theater where they put on plays and schedule lectures. Behind Main Street there are grand, well-kept Victorian houses adorned with porches, turrets, stained-glass windows, each with a driveway leading back to a large barn. There are also contemporary homes of no distinction at all, and a host of run-down, multi-family residences that bespeak ill fortune, most likely the outer signs of addiction, something he's never had to battle himself.

But his struggle, he is beginning to understand, might have the same root cause: an isolation of the spirit. Though he thinks of her with longing, he knows he isn't in any shape to have a relationship. Rachel must have intuited that. That's why she hasn't called. Right now, the only person who can tolerate him, and vice versa, is his fuck-buddy.

Why do some people suffer that isolation while others don't seem to feel it at all? He doesn't know. A question better suited for Donna.

He closes on the land in the last week of December. Linda handles the transaction in an inner room at the real estate office. Afterward, she takes him out to lunch. "It's official business, you're my client," she says as they walk into the most public place in the village, The Chili Hot.

Rubiat sees Walter at the counter and waves. They sit at a small table in the back, both ordering without looking at the menu, and when Walter stops by their table on his way out, Rubiat says, "I'm a landowner as of an hour ago."

"Congratulations, though what you want with it beats me.

But who can tell? Maybe you'll strike oil." The old man tips his cap and shuffles off.

Linda flips through the metal pages on the old-fashioned, table-side juke box. She puts in a dime and chooses a song and the tinny sounds of Nancy Sinatra singing, "These Boots Are Made for Walking," come out of the speakers. "It's not exactly how I feel, but I just wanted music to cover our voices. I'm ending it, Rubiat. He gave me an ultimatum. He knows, I don't know how, but I guess it's time he and I patched things up. It's been a lot of fun. You're a beautiful man and I'm going to miss you." She pauses. "You want some advice?" She lifts her sandwich, eyes on his face.

"Do I?" he asks as nonchalantly as he can.

"Don't waste your life like I did. I married the wrong person and did my thing on the side. I thought it wouldn't matter. I thought nothing would touch me. But I have to tell you, it trips you up. So, get it right. Get with the right person. That's what I want to say to you." She takes a few bites and puts her sandwich down. "Now, I'm going to stand up. We're going to shake hands, and I'm going to walk out. I'm not going to turn around. I'm going to walk into the rest of my life and I'm going to be a real partner to my husband from this point forward. I'm just going to take a breath first. Okay, kiddo," she squeezes his hand, "good luck to both of us."

He watches her walk to the register, a sexy woman with a body he has enjoyed, but a person he never knew, never was even curious about. The song ends and he puts in another dime to play it again. It's good cover for sitting at a table by himself in a town that watches his every move. But now he owned Poag's Hole.

40

Everywhere he looks something green pokes up from bare ground and leaves bud on all the branches. Macy has met the other dog who is often in the park at the same time he is; the dog's name is Samsa, the owner's name is Lindsey.

"Have I seen you at the co-op?" she asks one evening when the sun is setting over the houses west of the park.

"I'm the guy they hired to be the new manager. You're a member?"

"Have been for a long time. Actually, I was one of the people who applied to your job."

"Really? I'm sorry, you must have been disappointed."

"I was relieved, actually. It would have been beyond me, totally beyond me."

As they talk, the two dogs growl and sniff, then Samsa breaks into a run and Macy goes after him.

"Well, it's beyond me too. It's a challenging job." He isn't sure how much he should say. "I thought it would be easier than my old job, but I guess I was naive. It's different, but not easier. Politically, it's harder."

"You're the one who came from that big co-op in the city. I remember. They were kind of surprised you were interested."

"They discussed the other applicants?"

"Oops. Dammit, I always put my foot in my mouth." She laughs nervously, tilting her face up to the sky. "It's a beautiful evening, did you notice?"

"Are you changing the subject here?"

"Shit. Well, I have to, you see because I'm a terrible liar. So that's not an option." She looks after the dogs, then back at him. "My foot's still in my mouth and now there's only one way to get it out. Want to sit down? The dogs have disappeared."

"They're behind those trees. I saw a tail wagging." He whistles for Macy, but the dog ignores him. "Somehow, he always knows when I don't really mean it."

"The two of you seem kind of made for each other. Oops! There I go again. I mean, just in a feeling way, nothing really definite, not looks or anything."

Dusty can tell that this woman, who is exceedingly pretty, is hopeless at any kind of conversational strategy. She simply says what's on her mind. "You're going to tell me what you know, aren't you?" He's surprised she doesn't take offense.

"All right. I'll tell you the whole story." The wind moves through her hair, it reddens her cheeks, and he feels as though he's sitting next to a spirit of nature. Even her voice seems unearthly, but that's because it's soft, searching, not really sure of itself. "So, this is how it went. About six people applied, maybe seven, I don't really know, but everyone was qualified, or at least somewhat. Me, for instance, I had many years there as a member. And I think other people were like that too. But the person who was the most qualified had an issue that got in her way. I won't say the name of this person, but no one on the board wanted her in that position because she has zero, I mean zero, public relations skills. She's been a member for a long time and is very outspoken. She alienates people, and they knew if she didn't get it, she would make the new hire's life miserable. So when that got out, I withdrew my application and I guess most, or all of the other people did too. So, they decided to go outside the community. They knew they had to find someone who had exceptional qualifications in order to justify passing this person over. And that person was you!"

"I think what you're telling me is that they set me up. I was the fall guy."

She touches his hand. "No, Dusty, I wouldn't say that. Oh no, don't think that. It was just a delicate situation and your experience was what they needed. This person is formidable, and they thought your experience would give you a kind of armor."

"I know who we're talking about, by the way."

"I'm sure you do, but I'd rather not even say her name because, well, it's kinder if you don't, isn't it? Listen, I made a big
pot of chili and I have cornbread ready to go in the oven and
I live over there, that house with the red roof? Second floor.
I feel awful. But maybe, if you haven't had dinner, you would
come over? Do you think you could?"

The wind lays a strand of hair across her face.

41

A knock on the door of her studio. It's a tentative knock, so she knows it isn't the landlord. She hasn't paid rent in two months. Foolishly, she'd used the Citibank money to pay off her credit card and now she's hurting. Soon, once the boxes are finished, she will make good on everything, the rent, the bills, and still have money left over, even after the gallery's cut.

Another tentative knock. "Who is it?" she calls.

"It's Arthur, next door. Are you busy?"

She opens the door to his beaming, stylishly ragged figure.

"I felt so bad for falling apart back then, and you were so gracious and understanding."

"Oh no, that wasn't a problem, I was happy to have your reaction. Come in! Can I make you some tea? Sit down! Let me put on some water. How are you doing?" He seems relaxed, at peace, though she does notice that his eyes are still a bit red. He's holding a big paper bag. "The chairs are over there." She points to a stack of cheap plastic lawn chairs in the corner. "But look around if you want, though I should warn you, everything's in process right now, just fragments."

He looks at the drawings she has pinned to the wall. She has decided to limit her palette, but stay away from clichés of death, like the colors white and black, and concentrate instead on the feelings of the witness: yellows, reds, oranges, all at loud intensities. She wants a tangle of shapes, bends, twists, extending into a distance, but also partially obscured, emerging in one place, hidden in another because the witness is always shut out of the full experience; the witness sees only the immediate, the backstory she has to imagine. She's been using drawings to work out the color and texture vocabulary, and to her, right now, they seem too accidental, without design or intention. She has to play around a while more because right now, she's not sure how to give it authority, or what she thinks of as sharpness.

"These are all just starts," Rachel says when Arthur turns away, "so you don't have to comment. But sit. Is herbal okay?"

He takes two chairs off the stack and sets them in the center of the studio facing each other. "I have a partner," Arthur says. "Actually he's my boyfriend, and we design clothing. We also make accessories and I thought you might like one of these." He is pulling a long, thin scarf out of the bag. It has striped panels in red and yellow with pale pink squiggly lines. "I just wanted to give you something because I was such a mess then. Here, try it."

"Oh my god, it's utterly beautiful! Wow!" She wraps the soft, silken fabric around her neck, feeling its warmth right away. "You didn't need to do this. I was in fact honored that my pieces got that reaction. I mean, I'm sure it wasn't fun for you, right?"

Arthur doesn't answer and then he says, "This is kind of hard to admit, but—"

Overcome with feeling, Rachel exclaims, "It's so nice to know you're across the hall! But I interrupted, sorry."

"Have you ever lost someone you're close to?"

"Not really," she says. But then she corrects herself. "No, I haven't."

"There's this big, sloppy feeling and it just builds and builds inside of you, expanding, taking over, and it's such a relief, finally, to cry. It's like puncturing this huge, unwieldy balloon that's inflated in your chest, and when you cry, you feel it contract back to something manageable. So, the truth is, I'm giving the scarf as a way to say, thanks, I needed that."

"I will love wearing it. In fact, it reminds me of someone I've lost track of. Wow, clothing, how wonderful! Have you had your business for long? How's it going?"

"We're just starting, really. My partner's into fashion and I'm a fabric designer so we, so to speak, melded our talents."

"And what's the empty bowls thing? The celery?"

He looks confused, then he remembers. "Oh, right! It's a

charity. It fundraises for this organization that runs food pan-
tries. Ceramic artists donate the bowls that the soup is served in
and I donate the cloth napkins at each place setting. We put on
a dinner that costs mucho dollars to attend and people have a
good time while we serve them a good meal. It's basically chick-
en soup, salad, and rolls that a bakery donates. Plus wonderful
desserts. It works well, actually. It raises a lot of money and the
participants have a good time and get a beautiful bowl and cloth
napkin and they've contributed to a worthy cause. Like, maybe
you could create the invitations. Little paintings that people
would want to take home and frame. I'll tell you when the next
event happens. They're like, every two months."

"Sorry," Rachel says quickly, "I'm in the middle of a big
project right now. I'm barely making it myself, so I can't do
it right now. But later, I would like to. Later, I'm sure I'll be
available."

Arthur stands up. "I don't want to keep you, speaking of
being busy, I just wanted to pop in and give it to you."

She walks him to the door. She wants to hug him, but hesitates, and that's when he puts his arms around her and squeezes
her close. "Actually, you remind me of that sister."

"You have others?"

"Three, but she was my favorite."

It's only coincidence that he gave her a long, thin scarf like
Rubiat's, but even so, wrapped around her neck it makes her
feel stronger. And when she faces her wall of starts, she sees
some things she'd like to develop.

42

Everyday Rubiat walks on his land. He sees red-tailed hawks and red foxes. One day he sees a fox with something in its mouth. It looks big enough to be a chicken, and maybe it is, maybe he's raided a hen house, and is on his way to feed kits tucked away in a den. It's early spring. The creek is full of snow melt and as he walks, the wind tears through his jacket. Even when it's raining he goes out to his land, ownership not allowing for days off. He wants to know it completely, in all weather, even in the miserable spring snowfalls that make everyone at The Chili Hot grumble. He doesn't like parking on the road, so he pulls into the old driveway where a house once stood, leaving tire tracks and soggy footprints, signatures of his presence.

Sometimes in the evenings he visits the library across the street and reserves time at a computer. He keeps track of Rachel's career; he has looked at her work on a gallery's website. He's read about the boxes at Citibank and finds out that the opening to celebrate the finished installation was last week. Would he have driven down if he'd known? Probably he would have, and feels relieved he didn't have that temptation.

It's a lonely time. He thinks he might benefit from another session with Donna, something to break the utter isolation of his soul, but then he decides to use what he has, which is the land. He follows deer paths, sees an eagle sitting at the top of an evergreen tree, a turkey vulture sweeping over the field. He finds dirt trails of burrowing moles, sees robins in the treetops, hears their calls. He knows he's a beginner and tries to look closely, see everything. Growing up in a city, he lacks even the basic knowledge any country kid gains when he learns to hunt.

He talks to Walter every day. He talks to his customers about the weather, the roads, and the specifics of why they called him.

The servers at the Hot know him by name, and bring him his order without having to ask, but about himself—who he is and what he has done—he stays quiet. He's celibate and quiet. He exists; that seems to be enough.

When he sees the name, Solomon Vetterman, on his phone he doesn't recall who he is. But when he returns the call and hears the gravelly, smoker's voice, he remembers the wet basement and the book on the table called *Falling Water*.

That's the reason for his call. He's driving there in two weeks, on a Saturday, and invites Rubiat to come along. They can do it in one day, or sometimes Solomon stays in a motel outside of the city, it's cheap, two double beds to a room. Solomon coughs. He says, "By the way, there's nothing more to that suggestion except that it's a lot of driving for one day."

Rubiat recognizes the gesture of friendship and tells him he'd like to go.

"Excellent," Solomon says. "We'll work out the details later."

43

Dusty is getting tired of hearing himself talk about his girlfriend. *She's going to come down. But she has this commission. She's really busy.* He's starting to wonder if it will ever happen. How could she be so busy and so completely broke? It's an excuse. She can afford a bus ticket, what was it, fifteen dollars? He'll drive up and get her. But no, the boxes, the boxes.

He kicks himself for not going to the opening at White Pillars or Citibank. But he also knows he would have felt out of place with all those artists. Plus, they were on weeknights: too far, too late. But now he feels guilty and wonders if this not coming down is her punishment. Well, fuck her. If she can't understand he might be busy too, that's a problem. He stops calling and invites Lindsey and her dog over to his house for dinner.

It's a warm spring evening and she arrives with a salad and dog treats, following him up the stairs like a person who already knows the place, hanging her coat on a hook next to his, setting her bags on the floor, shoes next to them. "Show me."

He laughs. She laughs too and then she says, "What are we laughing about?"

"I'm laughing at you because you're so…how can I say it?"

"I don't know, Dusty." She throws her arms up and walks around his foyer admiring the details: the high baseboards, the large window, the wide plank flooring.

"You're so refreshingly uncomplicated. My girlfriend in New York, well, nothing's ever simple. For one thing, she never laughs."

"That's not good. But then the opposite isn't good either and sometimes I worry about that, that I laugh too much, but then I think, too much for who? Not too much for me. I always try to be optimistic."

"Me too," Dusty says, and he takes the bowl of salad she brought into the kitchen. The dogs are standoffish. They sniff, growl, and lunge at each other, keeping a wary eye when they settle down to chew their biscuits at opposite corners of the room. "Do you want wine?" he asks. "I got a bottle just in case, though I did notice that you didn't serve it at your house."

"Yeah, well, to tell you the truth it was intentional. But you have it, go ahead, I won't mind. I've been sober for a while and it won't bother me."

"Oh really? For like how long? Here, I put some appetizers and things in the living room. Come, sit, relax, would you like some juice or something, or just plain mineral water, maybe, what can I give you to drink?" Holding a beer, he is suddenly filled with nervousness. What can he give her? How can he make her feel at home?

"Can I look in your fridge?" she asks, walking in the wrong direction, away from the appetizers and into the kitchen. He finds her standing in front of the open door, the yellow light of the refrigerator bathing her, outlining her form. She reaches in, grabs a mineral water, a lemon, and says, "This is what I'll have."

Something seizes him. His brain splits down the middle, the present on one side, and a future when her figure, standing at an open refrigerator door, will be commonplace. She finds a small knife (she's chosen the correct drawer), cuts the lemon, squeezes it into her glass and pours the fizzy water over it. He watches and knows with certainty this will happen not just once in his life, but over and over.

But then the door to the future closes and he finds himself following her into the living room, passing the two dogs chewing their biscuits, Macy making a low, warning growl, her dog, Samsa, growling in answer. "His first name must be Gregor, right?"

"Of course! How good of you to figure it out! It was a moment of despair, really, when I named him. I wanted to remember that anyone, dog or person, could, without warning, wake up one day and be transformed. It's my favorite book. Every few years I read it. Do you have something like that? A book that means a lot, that maybe you take as a sort of letter the author wrote to you alone?"

"I'd have to think about it, I'm not sure."

"Then you don't. Because if it's not right there you probably don't. Maybe you're really comfortable in your life. I'm not. I don't really fit. Which is why the *Metamorphosis* attracts me."

"How do you not fit? You seem so, I don't know, so easy with yourself."

"That's a good question, absolutely the kind a therapist would ask. Not that I'm seeing one, not at the moment, but I think I could really be helped if I did. Hmmm." She cocks her head to the side, thinking. "I guess it's hard to put it into words."

The light outside the window is softening, the tree filling with starlings. They whoop and chatter, noisy trumpeters of evening.

"Can I tell you something?"

"Sure." But he says it nonchalantly, taking a sip of beer.

"No, I mean really tell you something."

So, he adds, "I'm all ears."

"That's not really what I mean. This isn't talking to entertain. I want to really tell you something."

There's a pained expression on her face; her eyes search him, but without amusement, without the usual fun.

"I have an idea," he says. "Let's get the dogs and walk over to the park. You can tell me there and then we'll come back and eat. I always think trees help, don't you?"

"Brilliant," she says.

At the park the branches of a pin oak are massed with more starlings; it's such a large flock the chattering, busy birds create the illusion of a moving treetop. The dogs go off, friends now that they're in neutral territory, and he and Lindsey walk through the dewy grass, the cold spring air whipping their faces. "I tried to kill myself in high school. Pills. I didn't take enough. Obviously!" She doesn't laugh. "I don't know why I did it, and I went to therapy for years. There didn't seem to be a single reason, just a feeling, really, that I wasn't going to make it, that everything was beyond me. Total despair. Very painful. Then I started to drink, sort of a slow suicide, but something pulled me back from that, I'm not sure what exactly, but I guess I have kind of a braking system inside me. I can always lift off, find another spot. I started going to AA which has really helped. So now, I'm just trying to be outward focused. The trees, the sky, the birds, the dogs, dinner with you. I feel happy. That's what I want to say. I'm happy to know you. I mean, you have a girlfriend already, you've mentioned that a few times, so I know you're not available, but it doesn't matter. I'm happy to know you. I feel, sort of, like I've always known you and it's nice to reconnect. I don't know if you believe in past lives, do you?"

They're standing so close he simply puts his arms around her and whispers in her hair: "Thank you. I'm glad you weren't successful and I'm happy too, really happy, to know you." As he says it, he decides he'll end things with Rachel. This is the woman for him. Her cheeks and the tips of her ears are reddened from the wind and her hair is blowing. She twirls around, throwing her head back, opening her arms, shouting, "Life is so grand! Isn't it? Isn't it?" as above them, starlings flutter nervously.

44

Vetterman chooses the route and does the driving. He prefers the long way through the state forests of Pennsylvania. The miles and miles of unbroken green is a better preparation, he says, than the interstate. The house demands it.

They are in the forest for hours, the conical shapes of evergreens piercing the sky as they chat about unimportant things and listen to music. When the news comes on the radio, Vetterman changes the channel. "Reality we don't want," he says, fiddling with the dial till he finds music again. But there are long stretches when the radio picks up nothing and they talk easily, though it is Vetterman who does most of it. He tells Rubiat about the job he used to have, the house he used to live in. And then he says, "The first time I saw Falling Water I was questioning everything, and especially art. I was nineteen. My brother was in medical school, my mother worked as a dental technician, and my sister was training to be a midwife. My father, well, he never talked about it much, but he made a lot of money and essentially, part of what he did was manage portfolios for a couple of retirement funds. The whole family was doing important things and I wondered, am I crazy? Because at that time I was going to the university and had wandered into the art department, you see. And that's where I stayed. I wanted to be a painter. I was doing bad Magritte knockoffs, narrative paintings where everything looked normal until you noticed that it wasn't. A house floating at the tops of the trees, that kind of thing. When I saw Falling Water I was amazed. How could somebody, and not just a schlump, but a respected, world-famous architect, decide that a house could indeed float? That's the thing. I wanted to discover how he had the balls to do it. And that led me to art history. What were the precedents, that kind of thing."

"Did you get your answer?"

Vetterman laughs. "He had the balls because he was an arrogant bastard and he had a client with unlimited funds." But then he turned serious. "Actually, I think it was stubbornness mixed with romanticism which is a powerful, potent blend. For instance, what he did with this house, he created a new way of living. Nothing short of that. Because, see, what the house does, it eliminates the boundary between interior and exterior. That's amazing, and absolutely radical! For instance: There is as much unroofed living space as there is roofed living space so the inhabitants can be outside as much as inside. He ignored the tradition and that changed everything. It did, it really did. The people in the house were not separate from the landscape. They were part of it. I guess what it did is, to go back to the art thing, it made me understand that an artist can be a force for good, just like a doctor, a dentist, a fund manager. In fact, maybe an artist does even more because art, architecture, whatever, creates the spaces we occupy. A painting on the wall makes the room feel a certain way, a sculpture on a table. They're dynamic presences, as dynamic as a person, maybe even more dynamic. Actually, definitely more dynamic."

They park at the side of the road and all Rubiat can see, at first, is an unbroken vision of trees. And then he hears it, the roaring, plunging water, full of snow melt, rushing with spring energy, sending plumes of moisture into the air. Then, improbably, the walls of the house enter his line of vision.

They haven't approached it as visitors are supposed to; they see it from the back first, sneaking in from the forested side, illegally. Vetterman worked the route out years ago, and now, with Rubiat in tow, they squeeze between strands of barbedwire fencing, picking up the pathways made by groundskeepers to arrive at a building that doesn't interrupt or overpower the landscape but seems to be an organic part of it. It's perched on rock, its horizontal structure reaching out to the trees, all of it polite and respectful, like a great winged bird roosting in that spot temporarily. Though it isn't temporary at all. The house, from a different standpoint, looks like a grand lateral stairway climbing up the hillside, firmly rooted, a permanent presence despite its airy, open aspect, despite the appearance of fragile tenancy.

They sit in the living room for a long time, looking out the windows, walking through the hatchway and down the steps to the stream below, over and over, marveling and entranced. They spend a long time outside the house looking up at the supports, speculating about the decisions the architect had made, both of them agreeing that the most unusual aspect was the bold, uncompromising fantasy of it. Of course, the wealth of the owners was a factor, but it was also, they agreed, the architect's pragmatism that allowed his vision to be realized. He hadn't attempted the impossible. From the beginning, the fantasy was tempered by the realities of construction.

That night in the motel they watch the news and then lay on their separate beds talking. Solomon sips from a small tumbler of scotch; Rubiat drinks tea.

"That's probably why I bought a house with a wet basement."

"Why?" Rubiat asks, not following.

"Proximity to a stream. Hell, I've been making the pilgrimage to Falling Water now for probably ten years. Someday I'd love to build my own place, you know, try to find my own watery vision."

"You don't crave cigarettes anymore?"

"Well, that's a non sequitur if I ever heard one. Why'd you ask?"

"Watery vision, I guess, your wet basement. When I came out to your place you'd just stopped. You seemed fidgety and nervous, but you seem calmer now."

Solomon laughs. "I still miss it. But the worst's over. I've evened out, sort of. What about you? Do you rent or own?"

"A couple months ago I bought five acres with a stream and I want to build some kind of structure. Close to it, but now, I'm thinking, why not over it? I'm totally inspired now."

"I'll loan you my books. Maybe, if you're up for it, if you want it, I could help. You don't know me very well, Rubiat, but I'll behave. I won't be bossy. Edith always complains. It's the effect of teaching. I think I'm right, always, and I'm fairly aggressive in offering my opinion. It's been hard on her. I impose, direct, explain."

"Actually, that's what I need. I would welcome your opinionated assistance."

"Fair enough," Solomon says. He turns off the light and soon he's snoring softly. The fan purrs in the heater under the window, the cold air slips through the cracks around the door while Rubiat, in his bed, lies awake, an image of a house floating in the sky, drifting toward him.

45

This time, Rachel decides to construct models out of cardboard before making the actual boxes. It will help with expenses. She'll make her mistakes in cardboard rather than wood, fabric, and other materials. The models help her work out the rhythms of color which of course saves on paint. But with the added time and lack of money, she becomes even more reclusive. She calls her gallery to ask if there's a possibility of getting an advance. She's used up most of her savings and every day there are threatening notices from utility companies in her mailbox. She's never been so delinquent, but once she gets to her studio, she's able to banish the outside world and work contentedly for hours, breaking only to eat cheap, simple foods: apples, peanut butter, crackers, carrots. She hasn't had meat in weeks, much less green vegetables or fish.

What provides nourishment is the work. Her tables are covered with sheets of cardboard painted in bright colors, mostly yellows, oranges, reds. Now she's adding the cooler colors to create a shift in heat and intensity, putting a gray next to an orange, cutting the gray into strips to layer over the orange with a cool blue dripping down from the top edge. She slots them into cardboard models and they become layers extending into a distance that she hopes will feel luminous. These boxes won't have silver wire, because now she sees another kind of barrier: time. There's a creeping dark shape progressing toward the luminous horizon but moving slowly. In some, it's more opaque and puddle-like, but in others, it has the shadowy suggestion of something upright, maybe human. It's never the focal center, but rather a glimpse of something stealthy on the side, transforming, shifting, but always advancing toward the steady beacon of a distant spot.

Another change: His initials have been subsumed in the energies of color. Here and there, remnants are visible, the pillar of the R, the laddered lines of the E, but overall, she has let the letters go. Early one morning, when the studio was washed in the hopeful colors of the dawn sky, she had realized it was sentimental to keep him caged in one identity. It would be like someone locking her into the definition of her name as middle class and American, when, in reality, it is only a shorthand for the immensity of who she is. So, she must let him have immensity too, and not insist on who he seemed to be, a man with Arabic forebears.

46

Mr. Barkan is very excited to hear that the work is going well and wishes he could offer an advance, but unfortunately, I'm sure you know how it is, the costs of installation and the number of other artists whose work he supports prohibits him. He's truly sorry." The dealer's tone is encouragingly sympathetic. "You have to realize that he has one of the most respected collections of contemporary art and you're extremely lucky to get this commission and I'm so sorry to disappoint you but, that's how it goes, unfortunately. You'll find, and this is true for many of the people we sell work to, that wealth is always tied up. It rarely means easy access to cash. These people are always cash poor, but I can assure you that when the pieces are finished, he will pay and you will be pleased with the installation. He never skimps on installation. And the gallery will insist on a professional photographer to document so you and we will have images we can submit to interested parties. The Citibank purchase and now this. I think you are well on your way and we know we can interest other collectors. Rachel, this is just the beginning. But I do have another call, so we'll speak again soon I hope."

They weren't that cash poor. A small advance, a couple hundred a month until the work was finished, that was all she had asked for.

Soon, Angela will come with dumplings and Rachel has to get ready. She goes out to the wine store, but she can't afford wine plus salad fixings, so she buys the wine and when she gets home and surveys her refrigerator, decides she will make steamed carrots. She mixes them with butter, honey, and dill; it was her mother's default vegetable dish, a staple of her childhood in western New York. She hopes Angela won't mind.

This time Angela brings three kinds: spinach/scallion;

ground pork; and three mushroom. She pulls the containers out
of her bags, takes off her coat, gives Rachel a hug, and then she
says: "Dietrich proposed. I told Lin Lin and she's ecstatic. She's
always been afraid I would marry a Chinese man and suffer
the same way she did. So, any non-Asian male is all right with
her, and Dietrich is pretty much the opposite: thick, balding,
German."

Rachel affects happiness, but the truth is that she feels betrayed. It's selfish, she knows, but she assumed they would be
single women together until they both decided not to. "You
said yes?"

"Well, I said probably. I told him yes would take a little more
time. But I gave him hope." Angela arranges the dumplings in
the steamer while Rachel sets the table. "Did you make salad?
Shall I put it out?"

"I made a very American dish instead, cooked carrots. It's in
the bowl on the counter." Rachel pours the wine and lights the
candles. "Probably," she repeats, feeling the alien word in her
mouth. Dusty's proposal had been so unwelcome she'd never
told Angela. Now, that long-ago evening returns to her and
she sees how much kinder *probably* would have been, even if it
wouldn't have been true. "What about the ownership thing, you
know, his fascination with all things Chinese?"

"It's gone. I'm Angela to him, Angela who happens to have
a Chinese grandmother."

"And your painting? He understands you'll need time in your
studio?"

"When I said probably, we had a talk about finances. And
I learned that a journalist makes a pretty good living. In other
words, he could support me if I wanted to be supported. If I
wanted to keep on working for the dumpling shop, I could do
that. But I couldn't work full time and be at my studio all weekend. He said, 'I don't want to be married to a ghost.' It would be
a huge change, but I've fallen in love with him, Rachel, and I'm
going to say yes. It has nothing to do with the money. I want to
be with him. I want to share my life with this person who is so

very different. Though I'm a bit worried about Lin Lin. I don't
know if she can manage without me. He says we'll get a bigger
place, she'll move in with us, but he doesn't understand. She's
never been out of Chinatown. She has her habits, her friends,
her shopkeepers. She has a full life there and at ninety-one she's
not very adaptable. I think I'll just have to visit a lot. How are
the boxes?"

"They're slow. It's really tight, but I think I can finish in time.
I'm working late every night."

"Teaching?"

"No, I'm in the studio till midnight at least. I haven't been
teaching since December."

"You must be exhausted. Those are long hours. Well, when
you're ready, if you want feedback, I'd love to see them."

"Thanks, but I'm still in the cardboard stage. Let me finish
an actual box and then I'd love that."

"Have you seen Dusty?"

"Nothing. Not since a very awkward evening. Going to visit
him is the last thing I have time for, and he hasn't been here
because I was so terrible, so awkward, so shaming. I think his
face still burns." Rachel tells her about the proposal in the busy
restaurant, the engagement ring that fit perfectly, the song she'd
learned for him. "I shamed him and I don't know if he'll ever
come back."

"Well, maybe it's for the best. You never seemed really en-
thusiastic. Did you find Rubiat?"

Rachel brings her up to date on the search, the shoe store,
his uncle, his mother, the lunch, even singing in the middle of
the restaurant. "He emailed me his phone number, because
after all that, the number his mother sent me didn't work."

"And? How did he sound?"

"I didn't call."

"Rachel! Why on earth not?"

"It's the boxes. Do you understand?" She's hoping that Angela will know, that she won't have to put it into words, but her
friend shakes her head. "I guess I missed something," she says,

and Rachel realizes that what she thought was obvious isn't obvious at all. "They're about him. He's what's inspiring this group of work. Or not him exactly, but the mystery of him, of that day I can't ever be free of. Don't you see? If I talk to him, if I get all my questions answered, I'm afraid I'll lose that vital thing. I mean, the not-knowing is necessary. If I lose it…who knows? I'll call him when I'm finished."

"That must have been quite a night!"

"Meaning?"

"To make him decide to disappear."

"I didn't tell you all of it. There was also the day after."

By that time, her windows have turned black and the two candles are the only light in the room. Everything feels hushed, the whole building leaning into the night. She imagines dark figures passing under the streetlights, lit for only a few seconds, footsteps tapping into the distance. Movement swirls outside while she stays still and someone on the first floor slams the front door. They've eaten all the dumplings and the carrots, which Angela loved, saying this is better than salad, we should have this as a side every time. They have even finished the bottle of cheap, too sweet wine.

Angela steps into the kitchen to make tea and Rachel listens to the sounds of someone else opening drawers and cupboards. She doesn't want to clear the table. She wants only to stay still. The dirty plates, empty glasses are comforting. She's been working for so many days she's hungry for this peace, this reprieve, but she's also scared to talk about Stony Brook. What had happened there is between her and Rubiat. She should never have brought it up. It's like Dusty's proposal, like his song: too much, too soon. She shouldn't have mentioned the awkwardness with Dusty either. That's private too. But this is her good friend, her confidant. What are the boundaries? Sex is private, bodies are private, but her history with this man is private too.

Angela brings two cups of tea to the table. "Your apartment is like an oasis, a little tree house in the wilderness of the city. I sort of dread leaving, but it's going on ten."

"Do you have to?"

"Well, I would need to be home by noon tomorrow. Lin Lin would assume I'm at Dietrich's. A sleepover?"

"I would love it," Rachel says. "You can't imagine how much I would love to do that."

They wash and dry the dishes, she loans Angela a T-shirt to sleep in, and then they sit on the couch listening to a version of "Let It Be Me" that Rachel finds on YouTube. And then Angela asks the question she's been dreading. "So, with Rubiat, what happened the next day? You never told me."

She says it quickly, she makes it a bold statement of fact without any details. "He jumped off a cliff at Stony Brook into the dry gorge."

"And died?"

Rachel shakes her head.

"No?"

"Why on earth would he do something like that?"

"Exactly what I've asked myself a million times. Why, after such a great night together? It feels like some kind of gesture meant for *me*, a slap in the face, kind of."

"You saw him do it?"

"With these eyes."

"That's scary. That's a scary person. But thank you for telling me. No wonder you're still fixated on him. No wonder you couldn't take Dusty seriously. Rachel, you have to talk to this guy. You have to find out what's going on with him. I've never heard of anything so strange. I can understand why you never told me, or at least I think I can."

"You do?"

"Yeah, with Dietrich, it's like we live in this other country, the country of us, which has its own history, its own timeline, and even, sort of, its own language. It's very, very private. So I'm not going to ask anything else. I want to respect that privacy, but, Rachel…" Angela stops talking and simply looks at her. "Rachel! How could you ever trust him again? I hate to say it, but is he insane?"

She laughs it off. But is he? Has she dedicated her art and really, her whole life, to a mystery that's been created by someone who is merely crazy? "I don't think there's a line dividing sane and crazy. I don't think it's so clear, ever. People wander back and forth. I mean, I don't know, obviously, but you have to put your trust somewhere, don't you?" But inside, she wonders.

47

The cold windy days of April roll over to May but the temperature doesn't rise. Heavy rains make the earth spongy with water as the stream, escaping its banks, spreads across the field. Frogs sound from all directions, some of them quacking like ducks, others trilling in harmony, and behind it all, the steady peeping of the peeper frogs, dense and operatic, saturating the loose evening air. His first thought is to build a cabin on stilts. It would stand above the stream and there would be a stairway, just like Falling Water, leading down to Poag's Hole.

By June, summer seems to have settled in, though there are days when the temperature drops abruptly, bringing cold nights. The waters have receded back to the stream bed and blossoming bushes and trees scent the breeze. June's airy sweeps of sunlight make the idea of an enclosed box, raised above the stream like a hunter's blind, casting its shadow across water and landscape, imposing order and symmetry on a wild space, feel repugnant and, as an amateur architect, Rubiat can appreciate the terraces of Falling Water that so cleverly contained functioning rooms. He needs much less space, of course, and he sketches out a pared-down version with one terrace, a stairway to the stream, and a windowed space that would be divided into bath, kitchen, and living room, with a bedroom perched above, similar to Rachel's turret. Solomon comes out frequently and they design Falling Water's cantilevered structure to fit this smaller footprint.

By July, they're discussing the placement of posts. They've learned that the stream is a wily creature, spilling its banks every time the rain is heavy, and they know they'll have to drill deep to find solid ground. Solomon is ready to go ahead with that plan, but Rubiat wants to slow down. He wants to apply for another loan, though getting a bank involved will bring in rules and regulations they might find difficult to accommodate. Could his salary alone support the project? There are so many details to work out, he realizes he must think everything through carefully. But it's only practical, this pressure. He is safe, the land won't make emotional demands, and the challenges presented by the project are like the challenges of plumbing; they have solutions, but he must take his time and discover the right ones. In perpetuity, but he has always lived in the moment, and as he casts forward in his mind, trying to head off the problems that may arise later, he feels grounded and solid, more so than ever before in his life.

Solomon is a good partner to have on the project. He's studied Falling Water and he understands its structure. He also knows its faults. The concrete must be reinforced with enough steel rods to prevent fractures and fissures from stress; he remembers that the engineer on the project clashed with Wright on that very thing and in the end, the engineer got his way. He has started smoking again and seems to treat the land as a boys' camp, a place where his wife's rules don't apply. Rubiat brings a tent and a sleeping bag and sleeps there on the weekends, spending long hours sitting in the darkness, listening, looking, trying to decipher the sounds and identify the constellations.

Solomon arrives with a sleeping bag one weekend and joins him. Sipping a beer, he talks about his marriage. "We've lost the spark. She'd be the first to admit it, but we carry on. We both know it's just a bump in the road, and actually, I know what's causing it. The smoking ban. She's the enforcer and that, for sure, precludes any sex, you know?"

Rubiat throws another log onto the fire. "Right, I can see that."

It bursts into flame and the orange glow silhouettes the two thin, rangy men. Solomon grinds his butt on the ground. He puts it in his pocket because he has the same reverence for the property as Rubiat. "I'm her project. That's the problem with not having kids. All her energy, and she has prodigious energy, goes to reforming the husband. Almost makes me want to have children, which is something I was determined never to do, but it would give her a focus, get her off my back. Rubiat…"

He can feel him waiting before talking again, knows something is coming.

"So, what's with you, man? What's happening in *your* life?"

"At the moment, nothing. I was fucking a married woman but then she reconciled with her husband. Just recently. So, I guess I'm looking."

"Hard place for a single man. You thought about that?"

"Yeah, but I'm taking a breather. It's okay. There's a woman in New York I used to know, but I did something really stupid, and I'm hoping to reconnect because, well, I think about her a lot and it was abrupt when we parted. I just, I don't know, hard to really know what's going on."

"Sure. Though with Edith, I have to say, she communicates." He laughs. "Sometimes I'd rather have silence. So much communication, it's exhausting, kills the mystery. Really, I don't need to be told everything. But you're a quiet guy, Rubiat, I like that."

"This woman in New York? We didn't know each other very long." He chuckles. "Not very long at all, but the first time I saw her, long before I spoke to her, I felt like I was looking at someone I already knew in a deep, kind of uncanny way. I've never had that feeling before. Hell, I was planning on leaving school, dropping out, it just wasn't for me. Being an artist, you know, you can't have any doubts, but then, when we got together, I felt differently. Like maybe I could do it. I can't, as it turns out. I like being a plumber, doing practical, rational, ordinary things, helping people in a straightforward way. But maybe I'll be an artist in this structure we're building."

Solomon stands up and unrolls his sleeping bag on the ground. "You have your inspiration, that's for sure."

"Right. And I have my partner."

"And your partner's going to sleep out here, under the stars. I know I'm going to regret it, because the dew might be heavy, but I haven't done this since I was a kid. You've got the tent to yourself, man."

And when Rubiat zips the flap he's happy to be alone.

48

Sometimes she stays at the studio till three in the morning. Walking back through the deserted neighborhood, hood up to hide her face, the only people she sees are the scavengers who go through trash cans looking for deposit bottles and cans. They wheel grocery carts bulging with plastic trash bags filled with their gleanings, workers cleaning up the discards of the careless. A decent haul means many streets, many hours. She admires their stamina, and always says hello when she passes one.

She's one month away from the due date and her food resources have dwindled. Now, she can't afford bread or cheese. She lives on cabbage, potatoes, eggs, cans of mackerel. It's okay. It fills her belly and there are endless ways of fixing them.

Someone must have let Angela into the building because there is a sharp rap on the door and there is her friend with containers of dumplings from the shop. "Put them in your freezer. They freeze well."

Rachel cries; she's so exhausted and her friend has brought enough dinners to last for weeks. They hug and when they step apart, she sees something different in Angela's expression, and then she remembers. "Is it still probably?"

When Angela holds out her hand, a small ring, delicate and beautiful, with an unusual ivory-colored stone circles her finger. "I said yes. I'm very happy."

Her first finished box waits for them on a table in the center of the room. It's three feet wide, eighteen inches high, and eighteen inches deep. She has put two chairs in front of it so they can peer through the window comfortably. What the eye sees is a long passageway. It feels longer than the actual depth of the box because at the sides there are panels of color, layered one after the other, each infinitely varied with a colorful, pattern-less composition. Some of the panels are more muted, others busy and vibrant. At the end, a window appears. It's shining, luminous, and beyond it, there is a meadow-like expanse with a bright orb of red beyond that. The viewer's eye travels down the pathway, pulled in by the suggestion of an outside place beyond the window. Only Rachel knows how the letters have morphed into the shapes on the panels; to a viewer, there is a lack of recognizable symbols, only the distance the eye must travel to arrive at the orb behind the window.

"It's a vagina!" Angela says. "Those panel-like walls are labia, the window at the end is the cervix, and the intensity beyond the window is the fertilized egg. Very sexy. I think the illusion of a journey, with the colors on the panels deepening as they go toward the window, is masterful, and up at the front, where you can see the thickness of the paint and maybe bits of fabric and paper, all of the stuff you've layered onto those sideway walls, or actually, they're like a line of doors, holds our attention and slows us down. There's lots to enjoy on our journey. But despite that build-up on the surface, they still feel labia-like, that is, fragile, delicate, like they need to be protected. It's such a protected, sacred space and the viewer feels lucky to see it. There's nothing death-like here. These are full of life, affirming, and about love, really. What I'm noticing is there's no evidence of how this has been constructed, no evidence of how these fragile walls are able to stand independently. The engineering is hidden so it feels very organic, not static at all, but changeable. Maybe the other boxes will document the way this changes over time. Do they?"

"They do. It's about time and change over time. I used to have this shape that would travel toward the end point, but I decided against it. I used to have his initials too, an R, an EL, but I decided it was too literal. I let them go and now it's just the language of color, line, shape, and space. I don't want to lose the question, what's beyond the window? So, I decided to trust the viewer, let her eye do the traveling, let her eye go where it wants to go." Then, suddenly, Rachel asks, "Do you want to have children?" It's a subject they've never discussed.

"German Chinese with red cheeks, blue eyes, and black hair. That would be something, wouldn't it?"

"They'd be beautiful," Rachel tells her and as she trains her eye on that red orb, she has a vision of her own lonely future. Angela disappearing into family life, Rubiat the mad performer somewhere beyond her reach, and Dusty in the reject pile.

"It's really, really powerful," Angela says. "I want to go into it again and again, but more than that, I want to stay there because after its intensity the outside world feels gray and pale, anemic almost. Definitely less interesting."

But maybe Dusty shouldn't be in the reject pile. She would call him. She would ask him to come.

49

He isn't sure what to do. He knows if he goes to New York to see Rachel they'll have sex and this new, delicate thing with Lindsey will be wrecked even if he never tells her about it. She's like the wind, fleeting, invisible, and ultra-sensitive. He wants to see all her moods, her gradations. Visiting Rachel would be going backward, when what he wants, what he needs, is to move ahead.

Her apartment is also on the second floor of a large stone house with its own stairway leading up from the front porch, but hers lacks the fine architectural details that his has. When he was leaving the last time they had been together, he had turned around on the bottom step and she was still at the top with the lighted kitchen behind her and Samsa at her side. Macy had stopped to look back too. And then she ran down after him, threw her arms around him, the dog coming down more slowly behind her, and said, "I just want to tell you something. Can we sit?" So they sat on the bottom step, Samsa licking their faces. Macy was already outside, waiting. That's the kind of dog he was; he waited.

"I think it would be nice to make love with you. And I know maybe you can't because of your girlfriend, but I want to tell you how good it feels to want somebody. It's been such a long time, like a rebirth or something, to feel this. That's all." She stands up, runs back to the top, the dog clumping after her, waves, and shuts the door.

The dark houses on the street watch from their many windows as a man overcome with happiness walks down the empty sidewalk through the glistening night.

He purchases a one-day round trip ticket for New York and thinks about the best way to have an honest talk. If he goes to her apartment, they will almost certainly end up in bed so he asks her to come to Prospect Park. They can walk and talk and he can gently, but firmly, close the door.

But is he certain? What if it doesn't work out with Lindsey? What if she's simply a self-destructive mess, charming but crazy? Does he really want to end it with a woman who is dependable and solid and has a true career? Because what does Lindsey do? Does she even have a job?

These are the things running around in his head and during his morning meditation it's hard to quiet his thoughts. He takes Macy for a walk and continues to pick away at the dilemma. But he has the ticket. He has to trust his instinct. And he has to trust Lindsey as well.

50

He told her to meet him under the arch in Grand Army Plaza. All the connections are good so Dusty arrives early. He stops at a food truck to get a coffee and croissant and watches the people streaming by, women pushing strollers, bikers and joggers, people with dogs on the leash. Then he sees her. She walks in front of the library, stops to wait for the light, and though he waves, she doesn't see him. She blends in with the Saturday morning crowd, a young woman with long straight hair, full breasts, hips bound by the tightness of her clothes, and a purposefulness to her stride as she crosses with the light and comes out in front of the others. Lindsey lacks that purposefulness. And Lindsey is thin and small breasted. Finally, Rachel looks up at the arch and then down at the lone person sitting on the concrete edge of a planter, and when she sees him, she slows her steps to gaze into his face. He stands up, they hug, and the heat radiating from her skin feels clean and good. "How was the trip?" she asks.

"Well, I've been up since five. Got a six-thirty train."

"You poor guy!"

They hold hands as they walk toward the park and when they come to Long Meadow, they find a bench and sit down.

"You're not staying over, are you? Because why else would we be meeting so early, why else would it be here, at the park. You never even showed me where you lived, and now I think I understand."

"Slow down there! Hold on! I'm here, aren't I? I want to see you."

"Okay, I'm sorry. Maybe we should keep moving. I feel restless."

He takes her hand and they stroll into leafy shadow, down crowded walkways, skirting small children running away from their adults. His dear old friend, the park. It soothes him, gives him courage.

But then Rachel interrupts the calm. "Sorry to do this, but I can feel you waiting to say something. So why don't you just say it?"

He peers into the speckled bower of an enormous plane tree. "Okay. Things have changed for me. There's a woman. I haven't slept with her, so this may be way premature, but I feel different. I feel committed in a way I've never felt before and I want to be truthful. I wanted to let you know how things are with me. I wanted to be honest and clear with you, I don't want to be, in any way, deceptive."

"Thanks," she whispers. Then she says, "It hurts."

He puts his arm around her, pulls her into him, but it's a fatherly gesture and she moves away.

"It's really hard right now. I'm lonely and alone and fucked over by all the men I know, which to be honest, are two. Plus, the collector who can't even give me a small advance."

"But other than that, your career's going really well, isn't it?"

"This is too hard, Dusty. I need to leave right now. So, I'm going to leave." She steps close and says, "Bye. It was fun." Then she gives him a kiss on the cheek and runs off.

Of course, all the way back to Philly he has second thoughts. Rachel is a strong, self-protective woman. Unlike Lindsey who clearly has problems. Or used to have problems, and now, seems to lack a self-protective instinct. Telling him she wanted to have sex when she knew he had a girlfriend, wasn't that opening herself up for disappointment? Or maybe it was being brave and honest. Or maybe it was being incredibly aggressive, trying to wrest him away from the other woman. Because what man could resist a confession like that? He feels too tangled to read, even to think, so he turns to the window and watches the highway.

51

Rachel knocks on the door across the hallway. No one is there. She knocks again, louder, just to make sure, and then she hears footsteps and the sliding of a lock. The door opens and Arthur is standing before her, looking disheveled. "Sorry, I didn't mean to interrupt. I just…" She can feel her face trembling. "Could I come in? Or, if it's not a good time, could you come over for a cup of tea later? I'm sorry, I'm interrupting you. Later would be fine."

Still, he says nothing.

"Were you sleeping?"

She sees awareness slowly enter his expression. He pushes the hair off his face and finally he steps back, gesturing her inside. She's never been in his space before, and from the dark, narrow hallway, an orb of daylight blooms in the distance.

"I guess I fell asleep. I was up really late and I was doing this painstaking brushwork and I guess I just dozed off. I always have trouble waking up. Takes me a long time, especially from a nap. Can I make you some tea?"

"Please."

"Come in, you can look around."

His studio is twice the size of hers. There are long rolls of paper hanging down from the ceiling with repeating patterns painted on them like wallpaper. Huge plants stand in pots about the room and there's a hammock strung between posts. There's a long table in the center with inks, paints, brushes, and a gooseneck lamp shining a strong light over the section where he had been working.

"This is a beautiful space. I'm so sorry to bother you."

"You're not," Arthur says firmly. "I want you to sit down. Here's a glass of water while the water's heating." He places a second chair for her to sit on. "Drink. Take a deep breath and tell me what's the matter."

"Oh god, I've just been dumped. And I wasn't even that crazy about him but he was my last resort. It's almost harder to be rejected by number two."

The kettle whines and Arthur brings back two mugs of tea. "May I ask then, who's number one?"

"Thank you, but it's a long and complicated story and I've barged in on you, so maybe I should just ask for a hug and leave."

"That's not going to work." The same firm, definite tone. "Here's what we're going to do. I'm going to work, it's very tedious pattern work, I'm just putting on the color, and you're going to stay where you are and tell me all about it."

"If you're sure. I know I would hate it if someone just barged in like this on me."

"Shut up and talk."

Rachel laughs, and then she tells him the Rubiat story. Arthur points out a new complication.

"It doesn't add up. Look, he's got a check for a few thousand dollars, at least, in his wallet, so he knew he was leaving school and he knew he'd never see you again. But then you have this amazing sex and it throws everything into question. All his plans suddenly look suspect. Maybe he's thinking he doesn't have to leave school. Maybe he should see this thing through, meaning, you and the assignment. Why then, would he do something so dangerous?" He looks up at her, dips his brush into a jar of water, loads it with a different color.

"Maybe he didn't want to admit he was wrong by going back to the bank and opening up another account."

"Really? He'd find it that hard to admit he was wrong?" Arthur goes down to the end of the table and pulls the paper toward him so he will have a new area to work on. "I know some men find it hard to admit they're wrong, but to die over it?"

"He never thought he would die. It was an impulse, a self-dare. He's arrogant and very sure of himself, that's what you have to remember."

"Okay, so he survived. Maybe he wasn't even really hurt. So why didn't he return to school, and to you?"

"I didn't tell you. I had his shoes and socks and I went back and left them on the path where I knew he would find them."

"What a motherly gesture. That's why he couldn't return."

"It is? How so?"

"When you're nineteen, twenty, you don't want your mother to rescue you anymore. You just want her to leave you alone. If he wasn't hurt, he would have been perfectly capable of going back to the spot where he jumped and getting them. Those little things your mother did for you when you were a kid: you don't want it anymore. I was the same way. Maybe for me it was doubly important because I knew I was gay, I knew I had to leave all that family stuff behind, at least until I got solid and okay with things, you know, okay with my body. You have no idea how important that was. Straights don't have that."

"But he's not gay. Or at least, he didn't seem to be."

"But all men, straight, gay, bi, they go through this."

"I was being overly protective? I should have left his shoes and socks up there where they were? Come on, I thought the man was injured or dead."

"But that's what you should have done. Only a mother bothers to think things through and second guess what a child needs."

"So now what? Do I answer his email finally, or do I just let it go? I mean, the guy jumped off a cliff when I was watching. I don't ever want to witness something like that again. I can't have that kind of craziness in my life."

"I agree. That makes total sense. But what do you *want* to do?"

Her lips begin to tremble and she can feel tears in the shakiness of her voice. "I want to know what he's doing, if he's all right. I just want him. The thing we had started, it might be something. Don't I have to find out?"

"Find him Rachel. Do it. Now get out of my studio."

"That's it then, that's what I have to do. Thank you, Arthur."

She holds them in until she opens her door. She doesn't turn on the lights. She slides down to the floor and wails. It's for every desertion in her life: Rubiat, Angela, and now Dusty. She's exhausted by the long hours and constant fears about money and the sound coming from her throat is not timid or reserved or careful. She doesn't care if someone hears. It's a catharsis she's needed for a long time, maybe since Stony Brook.

52

Her brother calls late that night and since she's still awake, she picks up the phone. Something is wrong, she knows it.

"I've fucked up. She broke it off. I told her, you know, I wanted to be truthful, and I said, 'I've dated someone else a few times, just to be sure, and it doesn't mean anything because it didn't work out.' And this monster took over. She screamed and carried on; it was unbelievable. I mean, I've never seen that side of her, though I knew she was emotional, but there was nothing I could say to assure her things were all right, and the irony is that the more she carried on, the more they weren't. But she was the one who ended it, thank god. I'm not going to miss her, not after that. I'm glad to be done. And I guess I'll just hit the pause button for now."

She manages a few sounds of comfort. And then she says, "Oh, Edward, I'm sorry. What happened with Ruby? You're not seeing her anymore?"

He sighs. "Didn't work out."

"Oh?"

"I don't know why, but I guess she's got someone else, though I'm not sure, really. It's okay and I'm okay. Don't worry. How are you?"

She laughs. "I just got dumped too." Shit, she was starting to cry. "Everything's too hard. I can't do it anymore."

"Rach, sweetheart. You okay? Want me to come down?"

"No, I'm not okay, but I'm too busy. Honestly, I can't spare a minute. But thanks. I just need a good night's sleep."

"I'll call you tomorrow," he says and the siblings hang up to face their empty lives.

53

On the first hot weekend in June, he drives to the land with drafting supplies. He wants to position the house in his mind and then on paper before finalizing the placement of the posts with Solomon. There's a car parked on the side of the road. He goes past it and pulls into the old driveway where he has parked so often the ground is bare. He's created a path from the driveway through the woods to the stream. He's cut down saplings, trimmed the lower branches on established trees, and mowed it with an old push mower he got from one of his customers. He's laid down bark mulch to define the path and then he's mowed the area where he puts up his tent. Though he keeps the mower on the land, he always takes the tent down in the daytime and stows it in his van.

As he draws closer, he hears laughter, splashing water and when he draws near, he sees that four kids are playing in the stream—two boys, two girls, high school age. One girl wears a one-piece, the other a bikini and the girl in the one-piece is chubby with short curly hair and freckles. The girl in the bikini is thin, blond, and clearly knows how stunning she is. The boys are in long shorts, one has a hairy chest and the other is hairless. They stand around the hole. Hairy slips into the water while the others sit on the rocks. "Dare you!" he says and the girl in the bikini dives headfirst and moments later, reappears. "That was scary," she says. "What if I missed it?"

"You'd crack your head open, that's what," hairless says, chuckling greedily and the girl in the one-piece cries out, "Don't do it again, promise me!"

"It's simple, what are you talking about?" Hairy climbs back on the rock and dives into the hole, but he doesn't reappear.

"Donny, don't play games, come on!" bikini pleads. "Donny, come on!"

He pops up, farther down the stream where the water is only as high as his knees.

Rubiat comes out from the trees.

"Hey, you guys," the one-piece warns, "someone's here."

"Hi!" bikini calls bravely. "You coming to swim too?"

"No, I don't think so. I'm the landowner."

"Since when?" hairy asks. "We've been coming here for years."

"Since January."

"Prove it," bikini says.

Rubiat laughs. "That's my mower under the tarp and you've never seen it mowed before, right?"

"We're really sorry," one-piece says, climbing out of the stream, walking over to grab her towel. "Let's just leave, you guys. I don't want to get into trouble. Come on, let's just get out of here. Maya!" she calls. "We're leaving. Hey, Maya, the bus is leaving!"

"There's another person?"

"My little cousin. My mom will kill me if we leave her."

Rubiat says, "Do you guys have somewhere else to swim?"

"Not really," hairless says. "There's a pond on my uncle's property, but it's full of leeches."

"It's really disgusting, you have to, like, pull them off your feet," bikini adds. "And sometimes they're really attached and then you have to burn them off with a match, which hurts."

The hairy one reminds him of himself at that age. Big feet, muscular calves, heavy eyebrows on a face that always stands out in a light-haired crowd. "We could make a deal," Rubiat says. "If I give you four—"

"Maya too, she's always tagging along. She's my punishment."

The others laugh.

"Maya too, so you five, if I give you permission to swim here, will you keep the other kids out and spread the word that it's private property and it's not allowed anymore? And if you come here to swim, don't leave trash. No cigarette butts, no beer cans. Is that a deal? It's not a place for drinking, no drugs, not even pot, understood?"

"Sure, that would be great."

Rubiat has been speaking to the hairy boy and he's the one who answers. Which is his girl, he wonders. Or maybe, they're too young to be paired off. Maybe they're all together. They promise to do what he asks and then hairless comes forward. "Thanks, sir. I'm Joey Sloan," and he holds out his hand. The other three do the same and he commits their names to memory. Becky Summers is bikini, Gertie Stone is one-piece, and hairy is Donny Malone. With more laughter and towel snapping, even some backward waves, they troop off.

"Hey, what about Maya?" he calls.

"She can walk home," Gertie shouts. "If you see her, tell her we left."

"Your mom's not going to kill you?"

"I can't be responsible. It's her own fault."

He remembers that too, how eager kids are to mete out punishment. They're vengeful gods, running an Old Testament world. Once they're out of sight, the sweetness of a strong sun fills his being. Birds sing from the thickets as he hauls rocks out of the stream and constructs a stool at a spot that will offer a good view of the property. His field stretches to the hills. At one time it must have been a hay field. The stream runs through it, cutting a channel that curves into the distance. If he positions the house over the hole, as he and Solomon intend, then the hole would be in perpetual shadow, and this wonder of nature becomes a basement. But where on the stream should the house be?

The first thing is to experience the hole himself. He saw exactly where the kids dove, and leaving his clothes on bushes, he wades into the stream. He stands under the waterfall and inches over to the hole, feeling the ground give way suddenly as he's thrown off balance by the pull of deep water. Then he climbs onto the rock above the spot and jumps in. The water sucks him down. He rises back to the surface and explores the edges to get a sense of its shape and size. The hole seems to be about four feet round. Someone has framed it with rocks so there are platforms to jump from. Or dive, though diving, as the girl said, is risky. He climbs onto the rock and springs off it, headfirst, tunneling into a narrow cave of water, sucked to its very bottom, and then thrust back to the surface. It's like nothing he's ever experienced, but the wonder of it feels familiar, and then he knows why, as he remembers his first dive off the side of the pool at the Y. He is still that nine-year-old boy, eager to disappear into water, ready to submerge himself into a new and challenging element. Rubiat dives many times. He enters a sliver of time that is past and present at once, a membrane of memory that has floated up into the present because even now, he is startled and amazed each time his body is sucked under. He is age twenty-six and age nine simultaneously. And then he knows: it is something he has to share. It can't be his alone. Of course. The thought sails into his mind with unusual certainty. His second realization is that the hole should be a walk from the house. It must be approached with intention, purpose, reverence. It's not simply a pop in the water, but a becoming, a transformative and formidable act.

He lays on the rocks so the sun can dry him and closes his eyes. There is just enough warmth for it to be comfortable. While the sun soaks into his skin he dozes off for a while, how long he doesn't know, but sometime later he hears rustling. A deer coming to the stream to drink.

"Where'd they go?"

A girl stands in the grass. He puts his hands over his groin, then sits up hunched over. His clothes are too far to reach, even the towel is out of grabbing distance.

"Are you Gertie Stone's sister, Maya?"

She doesn't answer, but apparently she is because she takes it as an invitation to come closer. "Oh shit, you're naked!"

"Would you mind turning around so I can get my towel?" She obliges and he says, "Okay," when he's covered.

"I found a fawn. It was just sitting in the grass by itself.

That's what their mothers do. They park them somewhere and tell them not to move no matter what. I kept it company."

"The fawn let you?"

She nods, comes closer. She seems almost as tall as her sister, but her hair is so blond it looks white in the sun and her body is thin and angular. "Your sister said to tell you to walk home by yourself. They left a while ago, so you should probably start out."

"Oh, that's okay, my aunt doesn't get home till dinnertime. That's when her shift ends. She works at the Hot."

"Chili Hot?"

"Of course, there's only one you know."

"Right."

"I found a really big waterfall. Want to know where it is?"

"Is there a hole under it, like here?"

"No, but it's like three times the size of this one. And there's a bigger pool."

"Could you show me?"

"If you get dressed."

"Of course, I was intending to get dressed."

"I won't look," she says, and when she turns again to give him privacy, he slips into his clothes.

Maya trudges through the stream with her sneakers on and he follows on land because he's wearing leather hiking boots and doesn't want them wet.

"It's really thorny up ahead. You don't have other shoes?"

"I didn't bring them."

"You're going to wish you had, I can tell you that."

She wears old clothes, a pair of wrinkled shorts and a T-shirt, both of them faded and torn. They come to a place where the stream forks. The smaller fork goes toward the hills, but the larger one, the one she follows, takes them into a grove of small trees growing above flowering brambles and vines. The air smells sweet, bees motoring in the white blossoms. He sees butterflies and moths, and then it becomes so overgrown he has no choice but to step down into the stream bed if he wants to follow the girl who never once looks back, but splashes ahead, because whether he keeps up or not is irrelevant. There are more rocks now and the stream levels out as the banks on either side grow steep. Maya has disappeared around a bend and his leather boots, heavy with water, slow him down. The rocks are so slippery with moss he crouches low, searching for handholds. The same viny, thorny plant with white flowers grows everywhere and now it rises in such profusion it drapes the trees. The stream narrows more and then he sees it disappear under a rocky cliff where a spume of water spills down. On the other side, Maya is lying in the pool underneath it, motionless and clothed, her arms and legs spread wide, as though she has fallen from the sky, the waterfall pummeling her.

When she hears him, she stands up. "You do it. Go ahead, lie down where I was."

He does as he's told, spreading his arms and legs out as she had, his face and chest receiving the spray, but the force of the tumbling water going to his belly. He is pounded into the earth, beaten by thousands of tiny fingers.

When they get back, he offers to give her a lift home, but without sensing the irony of it, she says she isn't allowed to accept rides from strangers.

"Well, we don't have to be strangers, Maya Stone, my name is Rubiat. I'm very pleased to meet you. Thank you for showing me that special place." He offers his hand and she shakes it gamely.

"I'm not Stone. I'm Haberman, but I live with the Stones in the summer because my mom works and I'd be cooped up in an apartment all day with nothing to do because my mom can't afford summer camp. I'm the summer boarder and they all hate me, which is okay, because then they leave me alone."

"Who hates you? Gertie and her friends?"

"Stupid Gertie and her stupid friends." She says it without

malice, only as a statement of fact, and looks up at him with such an expression of forbearance he thinks that maybe he is the only person in her life she can say this to.

"How old are you?"

"Fourteen." And then adds, defensively, "slow to develop, as you may have noticed."

"I didn't," he says, but in fact he has.

"I don't want any of that stuff anyway." And then, without saying goodbye, she bounds off, just like a yearling.

He eats the lunch he's packed and sits on his stool; the afternoon has confirmed that the house shouldn't dominate the stream in any way. It has to be separate because the stream has to be open for Maya.

In the evening, he lugs more rocks up from the stream and carries them into the field where he builds another stool. He sits facing south, watching the birds, the sky, the grasses. He sees how the breeze and the sun change the grasses and he thinks if he had it mowed every year to keep it a field he would always have the nourishment of this open vista.

54

F alling Water without the water?" When Solomon arrives that evening with a couple of beers and a sleeping bag, Rubiat tells him what he's decided.

"You're setting yourself up for trouble. Telling those kids they can swim? Someone gets hurt, you're going to be sued big time. You have to post your property and keep people out. That's what everyone does around here because it protects you from liability. Post the heck out of it. Own it, man, don't like, borrow it. It's yours. You paid good hard-earned money for it, or the bank did, and now it's yours. And the stream too. No question about it. And with the water rising and falling, a trickle at one point, a flood the next, it's a dramatic thing and it's your drama to enjoy. Just like Falling Water, your house will appear to float above it. Who cares about these kids? They're kids, they'll find other swimming holes. You can't tell me there aren't other places like this around here! You don't have to cater to them. You don't have to provide their recreation spot." Solomon pauses to take a sip from his can. "Own it! Enjoy it! You're paying the mortgage, the taxes, it's not public property." He lights his cigarette, and the scorched, tindery scent of smoke surrounds them. "Tell me I'm right."

Rubiat waits, he doesn't answer right away because he is reeling from the trespass of his friend's passion. The only person with the right to be passionate about this place is him. "I can't live my life in fear of being sued. I like these kids, especially Maya, and I'm not going to kick them off. Look, a house can float over a hay field. A hay field is golden under the sun, or it's like an ocean under the wind. It rustles, ripples, dances, depending on how the air moves. It's sexy and dramatic." That has no effect, so he says, "Look, when I was a kid, I had a public pool to go to. It meant everything to me. I wouldn't be who I am today without it. It was the best part of my childhood and there's no public pools around here, no YMCA. And this stream, with its deep hole, this is what they have, and they love it."

Solomon drains his beer, stubbs out his cigarette, puts the butt in his pocket, and stands up. "I guess we have a difference of opinion, but it's your land, your house. Why don't you think it over and contact me when you know." He picks up his sleeping bag and walks off in the direction of the road.

"I do know," Rubiat calls after him, but Solomon either doesn't hear or doesn't want to answer.

55

Rubiat, I apologize for the long silence. I've been really busy with a commission.

But it sounds like an excuse. She trashes that email and writes: *I had a commission that I was making work for that was about your disappearance, so strange as this might sound, I had to keep the mystery of what happened to you intact. That's why I didn't call. But now that I'm finished, I really want to talk to you.* She tells him a few things about herself and ends with questions for him. *Call me.* Then she clicks SEND.

56

That night, he pitches his tent in the field so the doorway faces south. He leaves the flaps open and at six the next morning the sun wakes him. He crawls out and stands up. There are ribbons of mist lying over the valley, floating in front of the hills. He takes out paper and pencil and sits on his homemade stool, drawing a house with two cantilevered terraces, an upper and lower, that float above the grasses, extending from a core of windowed rooms that contain the living spaces. There's a hatchway in the living room that opens to a small stairway descending to the ground. In the summer, the hatchway could be left open as a source of breezes; when it's closed in the winter it will be a source of light. This is the house he wants. Maybe you had to be as rich as the Kaufmans, or as famous as Frank Lloyd Wright, or as arrogant as his friend, Solomon Vetterman, but he is not going to claim the most magical portion of a stream as his alone. There are plenty of hay fields in Riverville. No one will mind his claiming of that.

57

On Monday evening he goes to the library to check his email. The next morning, he finds Henry at the Hot and takes a stool next to him at the counter. "I need a few days off."

"What for? Go ahead, order something, you want a coffee?" He holds a hand up for the server and says, "Dot, bring this man some coffee, will you?"

"I'll be back Wednesday. There's only a few jobs and all of them can wait. I've already called to let them know."

"You're not running after some little girl, now, are you?"

"A woman, yes, I'm driving down to the city to see a woman."

"And you're coming back Tuesday night? Well, bring her back! It's lonely up here and I don't want you abandoning me for some little girl who lives who knows where. You hear me?"

Walter turns toward him, the pouches under his reddened eyes more swollen than usual, the gray stubble of a hasty shave pocking his jowls. "Promise?"

Rubiat places his hand over the gnarled one resting on the counter. "Promise."

The van is his only vehicle and though the shocks are gone and two of the tires are close to bald, he has put off asking the old man to pay for repairs. He'll bring it up when he gets back. He's curious to find out if the monthly rent includes maintenance. It's something they've never discussed, and he is prepared for a circuitous answer as the old man finds his way to a decision. Cruising down route 86 toward the city, he imagines how the conversation will go.

So, you think the rental of the van and tools covers replacement and maintenance costs? I don't know. But we're partners and I like you and come winter, those tires will be no good. But the shocks, now, that's a tricky question because that's not seasonal. That's a liability all the time with the roads around here, pot-holed as they are, you slam down hard and you're likely to do real damage. So, for that, I'd say sure. We take it to my man, though, out on the Bolivar Road. Name of Henley. Just before the Tractor Supply. I'll call to let him know. That, most likely was how it would go because they've become friends, each looking out for the other, in the small ways you could in a shared business. And maybe the long and short of it is, the father he's never had is appearing now in his life as Walter Henry.

It takes six hours to drive to the city. He tries not to think, he wants only to watch the road and the hills and trees because he has to be empty when he gets there. He has to be empty of hope and expectations. And the thing he needs to be full of is himself, who he is, what he did to her, and how he's moved away from the impulse at Stony Brook. From impulse completely.

Before he goes across the George Washington bridge, he pulls into a gas station to text Rachel. Texting is laborious on his flip phone and it takes a few tries. No one cares about the old, dinged-up van parked behind the pumps, Henry Plumbing and Electric printed on the side panels, and so he takes his time, sends the message off, and then he pulls up to the line at the pumps, and facing the iconic skyline, he gets out and fills his tank.

I'm in the city. Where do you live?

An hour later, he parks close to the address she'd texted. It looks like an old school. He walks around it till he finds the entrance and then he calls, peering in at the filthy, graffiti-scrawled foyer. She comes down a set of wide steps, her body so fogged by the wretched glass she is simply a shape. When she pulls the door toward her and he steps through, one booted foot after the other, the leather still damp from his walk in the stream, he sees her. She is still the same, as though all the strange detours of time had never happened. "Rachel Normal Goodwin." He says her three names slowly. "I did a terrible thing. Do you think it would be possible, sometime, to let me tell you how sorry I am?"

She doesn't answer. But she says his name. "Rubiat El-sayem." Then her face breaks open, her composure melts, and he understands she's crying with relief because he is there.

ACKNOWLEDGMENTS

Special thanks go to Pam Van Dyk and Jaynie Royal at Regal House Publishing for their belief in this novel and their expert guidance into publication; to Marisa Silver for her feedback on an early draft; to Peter Selgin for his comments on a later draft; to David London, Ph.D. for his insights about a therapist's role; to Bill Coch and Martha Lash for their inspiring performance of "Let It Be Me"; and to the artist, Narcissister, for the mind-bending performance described in Chapter 1. I would also like to thank the painters in my family, my mother, the late Doris Staffel, and my daughter, Annabeth Marks, for their boundless generosity, over the years, in sharing their process. I am grateful, as well, for the nourishing exchange of ideas that took place every residency in the many years I taught in the MFA Program at Warren Wilson College; that exchange continues to inform and illuminate everything I do as a writer. And to Graham, Arley, and Annabeth for the great and sustaining pleasure of being my family.

BOOK CLUB QUESTIONS

1. Solomon Vetterman thought that Rubiat should enjoy the benefits of owning a property and if he wanted to build his house over the stream he should go ahead and do it and not consider that a bunch of kids would lose their swimming hole. Rubiat believed that he needed to respect the rights of other people and remembering how he had enjoyed swimming as a kid, gives the five friends access to the swimming hole. Who's right?

2. What's more important, her artwork or finding Rubiat? When Rachel chooses to delay contacting Rubiat because she wants to keep the mystery of what happened intact until she completes the boxes she's building for her commission, she's asserting her priorities. Was she right to do that?

3. Both Rachel and Dusty choose the unknown over the familiar and safe. How?

4. For Rubiat, how is guilt intertwined with love? Is this unusual or do you see how this twining operates in other people?

5. After reading this novel, do you think people do have a single causative factor, i.e. a particular emotion that is the foundation for all of their behavior? Does Rubiat? Does Rachel?